Horace Greeley, Charles Anderson Dana

Greeley on Lincoln

With Mr. Greeley's letters to Charles A. Dana and a lady friend

Horace Greeley, Charles Anderson Dana

Greeley on Lincoln
With Mr. Greeley's letters to Charles A. Dana and a lady friend

ISBN/EAN: 9783337122737

Printed in Europe, USA, Canada, Australia, Japan

Cover: Foto ©Andreas Hilbeck / pixelio.de

More available books at **www.hansebooks.com**

PHOTO-SCULPTURE OF HORACE GREELEY.

(By permission of the *Cosmopolitan Magazine*.)

Greeley on Lincoln

WITH

Mr. Greeley's Letters

TO

CHARLES A. DANA AND A LADY FRIEND

TO WHICH ARE ADDED

REMINISCENCES OF HORACE GREELEY

EDITED BY

JOEL BENTON

NEW YORK

THE BAKER & TAYLOR CO.

ROBERT DRUMMOND, ELECTROTYPER AND PRINTER, NEW YORK.

I do no

Mr. Lincol

and convo

useful me It b

~~they have~~ on my mind

~~~~ opponent of

in fairness

~~decided~~

it must have

~~acquired~~ i'q

reasonable

immunities

the same safe

~~and soft~~ ~~security~~

Rebellion

tranquillity

order and

PREFATORY NOTE.

THE great interest which every thing
that Mr. Greeley has written continues to
excite among multitudes of people, is the
excuse I offer for collecting these papers.
"How true it is," said a distinguished editor
to me, in speaking of Mr. Greeley, "that
that man never put his pen to paper without saying something."

His lecture upon Abraham Lincoln here
given, which has received the warmest encomiums, was first published in the *Century
Magazine*. It has a unique title to regard
from the fact that the conclusions it leads
to were a slow growth in Mr. Greeley's
mind, as Mr. Lincoln's fame and character
were in the mind of the public. It was

5

I do not suppose this logic convinced
Mr. Lincoln that the arrest, trial
and conviction of Mr. V. were wise and
useful measures of repressing con—, if they did
they have had no kindred effect
on my mind. Yet, I hold that the bitterest
opponent of the President and his policy must
in fairness admit that the case is virtually
decided that, if Government is to exist,
it must have power to suppress rebellion
against its authority, and that it is neither
reasonable nor possible to accord the same
immunities and maintain the same
safeguards of free speech and liberty
in the presence of a gigantic
Rebellion as in times of public
Tranquillity and unbroken obedience to
order and law.

PREFATORY NOTE.

THE great interest which every thing that Mr. Greeley has written continues to excite among multitudes of people, is the excuse I offer for collecting these papers. "How true it is," said a distinguished editor to me, in speaking of Mr. Greeley, "that that man never put his pen to paper without saying something."

His lecture upon Abraham Lincoln here given, which has received the warmest encomiums, was first published in the *Century Magazine*. It has a unique title to regard from the fact that the conclusions it leads to were a slow growth in Mr. Greeley's mind, as Mr. Lincoln's fame and character were in the mind of the public. It was

Mr. Lincoln's rounded career that brought
Mr. Greeley to see the wonderful man
whose life is so twined with the restoration
of the republic.

The letters to Mr. Dana, and those to an
intimate lady friend, not only cover rare
periods and incidents in Mr. Greeley's life,
but they show the *naïve*, unconscious mo-
tions of a mind never tempted to dissimu-
lation, and (in the privacy for which they
were intended) without motive to be other
than sincere. My own reminiscences can
only plead the value they gain from association with Mr. Greeley's name as justification
for their appearance in this volume.

I wish to acknowledge here my indebted-
ness to my friend, Mr. D. C. McEwen, of
Brooklyn, formerly an editor in the New
York *Tribune* office and at one time private
secretary of William H. Seward, for the use
of the Greeley manuscript relating to Mr.
Lincoln, and for very skilful and almost indispensable help in the preparation of a
copy of it for the printer.

J. B.

CONTENTS.

AN ESTIMATE OF
ABRAHAM LINCOLN.

Boston ... this lecture limited

Tuesday for July

says he has written either 1868 or not far

from that date but for . reason it did

not receive publication and it ...

was drawn delivered,

The Century for Sept. of the same year Vol. 42, 778

communications from two men who heard

Mr. Brady ...... id: one in Washington and

the other in New York

AN ESTIMATE OF ABRAHAM
LINCOLN.

THERE have been ten thousand attempts
at the life of Abraham Lincoln, whereof
that of Wilkes Booth was perhaps the most
atrocious ; yet it stands by no means alone.
Orators have harangued, preachers have ser-
monized, editors have canted and descanted ;
forty or fifty full-fledged biographies have
been inflicted on a much-enduring public ;
yet the man, Abraham Lincoln, as I saw
and thought I knew him, is not clearly
depicted in any of these, so far as I have
seen. I do not say that most or all of
these are not better than *my* Lincoln—I
only say they are not mine. Bear with me
an hour and I will show you the man as he
appeared to me—as he seems not to have
appeared to any of them ; and if he shall

be shown to you as by no means the angel that some, or the devil that others, have portrayed him, I think he will be brought nearer to your apprehension and your sympathies than the idealized Lincoln of his panegyrists or his defamers. Nay, I do sincerely hope to make the real Lincoln, with his thoroughly human good and ill, his virtues and his imperfections, more instructive and more helpful to ordinary humanity, than his unnatural, celestial, apotheosized shadow ever was or could be.

I shall pass rapidly over what I may distinguish as the *rail-splitting* era of his life. Born in a rude portion of Kentucky in 1809; removed into the still more savage, unpeopled wilderness, then the Territory of Indiana, in 1811; losing his mother and only brother while yet a child, and his only sister in later youth, he grew up in poverty and obscurity on the rugged outskirt of civilization, or a little beyond it, where there were no schools, post-offices few and far between, newspapers in those days seldom seen in the new and narrow

clearings, and scarce worth the eyesight
they marred when they were seen; the
occasional stump speech of a candidate for
office, and the more frequent sermon of
some Methodist or Baptist itinerant—earnest
and fervid, but grammatically imperfect,
supplying most of the intellectual and spir-
itual aliment attainable. He did not attend
school for the excellent reason that there
was no school within reach—the poor whites
from the Slave-States, who mainly settled
Southern Indiana, being in no hurry to
establish schools, and his widowed father
being one of them. So he chopped timber,
and split rails, and hoed corn, and pulled
fodder, as did other boys around him (when
they did anything); learning to read as he
best might, and, thenceforth, reading from
time to time such few books, good, bad,
and indifferent, as fell in his way, and so
growing up to be six feet four inches high
by the time he was twenty years old. As
no one ever publicly denied that he was
an obedient, docile son, a kind, indulgent
brother, and a pleasant, companionable

neighbor, I will take these points as con-
ceded.

About the time he became of age his
father made a fresh plunge into the wilderness—this time into the heart of Illinois,
halting for a year near the present city of
Springfield, and then striking eastward
seventy miles to Coles County, whither his
son did not see fit to follow him; but
having once already when nineteen years of
age made a voyage down the Mississippi
to New Orleans on a flatboat laden with
produce, he now helped build such a boat,
and made his second journey thereon to the
Crescent City; returning to serve a year as
clerk in a store; then heading a company of
volunteers for the Black Hawk war of 1832;
and next becoming at once a law student
and a candidate for the legislature,—receiving an almost unanimous vote in the only
precinct where he was known, but failing
of an election in the county. He had
already, since he became his own man,
obtained some schooling, and the craft of a
land-surveyor; he was twenty-three years

old when he in the same season became a captain of volunteers, a candidate for representative, and a student at law.

Let me pause here to consider the surprise often expressed when a citizen of limited schooling is chosen to fill, or is presented for one of the highest civil trusts. Has that argument any foundation in reason, any justification in history?

Of our country's great men, beginning with Ben Franklin, I estimate that a majority had little if anything more than a common-school education, while many had less. Washington, Jefferson, and Madison had rather more; Clay and Jackson somewhat less; Van Buren perhaps a little more; Lincoln decidedly less. How great was his consequent loss? I raise the question; let others decide it. Having seen much of Henry Clay, I confidently assert that not one in ten of those who knew him late in life would have suspected, from aught in his conversation or bearing, that his education had been inferior to that of the college graduates by whom he was surrounded. His

knowledge was different from theirs; and
the same is true of Lincoln's as well. Had
the latter lived to be seventy years old, I
judge that whatever of hesitation or *rawness*
was observable in his manner would have
vanished, and he would have met and
mingled with educated gentlemen and
statesmen on the same easy footing of
equality with Henry Clay in his later prime
of life. How far his two flatboat voyages
to New Orleans are to be classed as educa-
tional exercises above or below a freshman's
year in college, I will not say; doubtless
some freshmen learn more, others less, than
those journeys taught him. Reared under
the shadow of the primitive woods, which
on every side hemmed in the petty clearings of the generally poor, and rarely
energetic or diligent, pioneers of the Southern Indiana wilderness, his first introduction
to the outside world from the deck of a
" broad-horn " must have been wonderfully
interesting and suggestive. To one whose
utmost experience of civilization had been a
county town, consisting of a dozen to

twenty houses, mainly log, with a shabby little court-house, including jail, and a shabbier, ruder little church, that must have been a marvellous spectacle which glowed in his face from the banks of the Ohio and the lower Mississippi. Though Cairo was then but a desolate swamp, Memphis a wood-landing, and Vicksburg a timbered ridge with a few stores at its base, even these were in striking contrast to the sombre monotony of the great woods. The rivers were enlivened by countless swift-speeding steamboats, dispensing smoke by day and flame by night; while New Orleans, though scarcely one fourth the city she now is, was the focus of a vast commerce, and of a civilization which (for America) might be deemed antique. I doubt not that our tall and green young backwoodsman needed only a piece of well-tanned sheepskin suitably (that is, learnedly) inscribed to have rendered those two boat trips memorable as his degrees in capacity to act well his part on that stage which has mankind for its audience.

He learned and practised land-surveying because he must somehow live—not ultimately but presently—and he had no idolatrous affection for the wholesome exercise of rail-splitting. He studied law, giving thereto all the time that he could spare from earning his daily bread, for he aspired to political life; and seven eighths of all the desirable offices in this country are monopolized by the legal profession—I will not judge how wisely. He stood for the legislature, as an election would have enabled him to study regularly without running in debt; whereas land-surveying must take him away from his books. Beaten then, though he received the votes of nearly all his neighbors, he was again a candidate in 1834, and now, when twenty-five years old, and not yet admitted to the bar, he was elected and took his seat—the youngest but one, and probably the tallest member on the floor. He was reëlected in 1836, in 1838, and in 1840, receiving after his fourth election the vote of his fellow Whigs for Speaker. He had thus practically, when but

thirty-one years old, attained the leadership
of his party in Illinois; and that position
was never thenceforth contested while he
lived. When the party had an electoral
ticket to frame, he was placed at its head;
when it had a chance to elect a United
States Senator, it had no other candidate
but Lincoln, though under his advice it
waived its preference, and united with the
anti-Nebraska Democrats in choosing *their*
leader, Lyman Trumbull; it presented him
to the first Republican National Convention
as its choice for Vice-President, and to the
next as its choice for President, which
prevailed. Meantime, when a second seat
in the Senate became vacant in 1858, there
was not one Republican in the State who
suggested any other name than his for the
post. What was it, in a State so large as
Illinois, and a party that was justly proud
of its Browning, its Yates, its Davis, its
Washburne, and others, gave him this
unquestioned ascendency?

I would say, first, his unhesitating, uncal-
culating, self-sacrificing devotion to the

principles and aims of his party. When, a poor, unknown youth, he first proclaimed himself a Whig, Jacksonism was dominant and rampant throughout the land, and especially in Illinois, where it seemed to have the strength of Gibraltar. In 1836, Ohio and Indiana went for Harrison, but Illinois was not moved to follow them. In 1840, the Whigs carried every other free State, New Hampshire excepted; yet Illinois, despite her many veterans who had served under Harrison, or been born under his rule, as Governor of the Northwest Territory, went for Van Buren. Again, in 1844, Mr. Lincoln constantly travelled far and wide, speaking long and well as a Clay elector, yet the State rolled up a largely increased majority for Polk, and she went heavily for Pierce in 1852, likewise for Buchanan in '56. She never cast an electoral vote for any other than the Democratic nominee, till she cast all she had for her own Lincoln. I apprehend that throughout his political career Mr. Lincoln was the most earnest partisan, the most industrious, effective canvasser of his party in the State. Having espoused the Whig cause when it was hopeless, and struggled unavailingly for it through twenty years of adversity, his compatriots had learned to repose implicit faith in him beyond that which they accorded to any other man, Henry Clay alone excepted.

Our presidential and State canvasses are often most improvidently conducted. People wander to distant counties to listen to favorite orators, and swell processions at mass-meetings. They compel speakers to strain and crack their voices in addressing acres of would-be auditors; when, in fact, more effect is usually produced, so far as conviction is concerned, by a quiet, pro tracted talk in a log school-house than by half-a-dozen tempestuous harangues to a gathering of excited thousands. I perceive and admit the faults, the vices of our sys- tem of electioneering; and yet I hold that an American presidential canvass, with all its imperfections on its head, is of immense value, of inestimable utility, as a popular political university, whence even the unlettered, the ragged, the penniless may graduate with profit if they will. In the absence of the stump, I doubt the feasibility of maintaining institutions more than nominally republican ; but the stump brings the people face to face with their rulers and aspirants to rule; compels an exhibition and scrutiny of accounts and of projects, and makes almost every citizen, however heedless and selfish, an arbiter in our political controversies, enlisting his interest and arousing his patriotism. The allowance of a monarch, exorbitant as it is, falls far below the cost of choosing a president; but the popular acquaintance with public affairs diffused through a canvass is worth far more than its cost. That falsehoods and distorted conceptions are also disseminated is unhappily true ; but there was never yet a stirring presidential canvass which did not leave the people far better, and more generally, informed on public affairs than it found them. The American stump fills the place of the French *coup d'état* and the

Spanish-American *pronunciamento.* It is, in an eminently practical sense, the conservator of American liberty, and the antidote to official tyranny and corruption.

The canvasser, if fit to be a canvasser, is teaching his hearers; fit or unfit, he can hardly fail to be instructed himself. He is day by day presenting facts and arguments and reading in the faces of his hearers their relative pertinence and effectiveness. If his statement of his case does not seem to produce conviction, he varies, fortifies, reën-forces it; giving it from day to day new shapes until he has hit upon that which seems to command the hearty, enthusiastic assent of the great body of his hearers; and this becomes henceforth his model. Such was the school in which Abraham Lincoln trained himself to be the foremost *convincer* of his day—the one who could do his cause more good and less harm by a speech than any other living man.

Every citizen has certain conceptions, recollections, convictions, notions, prejudices, which together make up what he terms his

politics. The canvasser's art consists in
making him believe and feel that an over-
ruling majority of these preconceptions ally
him to that side whereof said canvasser is
the champion. In other words, he seeks to
belittle those points whereon his auditor is
at odds with him and emphasize those
wherein they two are in accord; thus per-
suading the hearer to sympathize, act, and
vote with the speaker. And with this con-
ception in view, I do not hesitate to pronounce Mr. Lincoln's speech at Cooper
Institute, New York, in the spring of 1860,
the very best political address to which I
ever listened—and I have heard some of
Webster's grandest. As a literary effort, it
would not of course bear comparison with
many of Webster's speeches; but regarded
simply as an effort to convince the largest
possible number that they ought to be on
the speaker's side, not on the other, I do
not hesitate to pronounce it unsurpassed.

I first met Mr. Lincoln late in 1848 at
Washington, as a representative in the
Thirtieth Congress—the only one to which

he was ever elected. His was, as appor-
tioned under the census of 1840, a Whig
district; and he was elected from it in
1846 by the largest majority it ever gave
to any one. He was then not quite forty
years old; a genial, cheerful, rather comely
man, noticeably tall, and the only Whig from
Illinois—not remarkable otherwise, to the
best of my recollection. He was generally
liked on our side of the House; he made
two or three moderate and sensible speeches
which attracted little attention; he voted
generally to forbid the introduction of slavery into the still untainted Territories; but
he did not vote for Mr. Galt's resolve looking to the immediate abolition of slavery in
the Federal district, being deterred by the
somewhat fiery preamble thereto. He introduced a counter-proposition of his own,
looking to abolition by a vote of the people
—that is, the whites of the district—which
seemed to me much like submitting to a
vote of the inmates of a penitentiary a
proposition to double the length of their
respective terms of imprisonment. In short,

he was one of the very mildest type of
Wilmot Proviso Whigs from the free States
—not nearly so pronounced as many who
long since found a congenial rest in the
ranks of the pro-slavery democracy.   But as
I had made most of the members my enemies at an early stage of that short session,
by printing an elucidated exposé of the ini-
quities of Congressional mileage ; and as he
did not join the active cabal against me,
though *his* mileage figured conspicuously
and by no means flatteringly in that exposé,
I parted from him at the close of the Congress with none but grateful recollections.
There were men accounted abler on our
side of the House—such as Collamer, of
Vermont ; Palfrey and Mann, of Massachusetts ; and perhaps Schenck and Root, of
Ohio—yet I judge that no other was more
generally liked and esteemed than he.
And yet had each of us been required to
name the man among us who would first
attain the presidency, I doubt whether five
of us would have designated Abraham Lincoln.

He went home to his law office after trying, I think, to be commissioner of the General Land Office under the incoming Taylor régime and finding the place bespoken; and thenceforth little was heard of him out of Illinois until the Northern uprising consequent on the introduction and passage of what is known as the "Nebraska Bill." He had hitherto been known as rather conservative than otherwise; this act had the same effect on him as on many others. He was henceforth an open, determined opponent of any extension of slavery to territory previously free. Thus he bore his part in the Illinois contests of 1854 and 1856; and thus when unanimously proclaimed the standard-bearer of the Republican party of that State in the senatorial struggle of 1858, he opened the canvass in a speech to the convention which nominated him, which embodied these memorable words:

If we could first know where we are and whither we are tending, we could better judge what to do and how to do it. We are now far into the fifth year since a policy was initiated with the avowed object and confident promise of putting an end to slavery agitation. Under the operation of that policy that agitation has not only not ceased, but has constantly augmented. In my opinion it will not cease until a crisis shall have been reached and passed. "A house divided against itself cannot stand." I believe this government cannot endure permanently, half slave and half free. I do not expect the Union to be dissolved--I do not expect the house to fall—but I do expect it will cease to be divided. It will become all one thing or all the other. Either the opponents of slavery will arrest the further spread of it, and place it where the public mind shall rest in the belief that it is in the course of ultimate extinction; or its advocates will push it forward till it shall become alike lawful in all the States, old as well as new, North as well as South.

Here is the famous doctrine of an "irrepressible conflict," which Governor Seward set forth four months later in a speech at

Rochester, New York, which attracted even wider attention and fiercer denunciation than Mr. Lincoln's earlier avowal. " Shall I tell you what this collision means ? " queried Governor S., with reference to the existing controversy respecting slavery in the Terri-tory. "They who think that it is accidental, unnecessary, the work of interested or fanat-ical agitators, and, therefore, ephemeral, mis-take the case altogether. It is *an irrepres-sible conflict* between opposing and enduring forces; and it means that the United States must and will, sooner or later, become either entirely a slave-holding nation or entirely a free-labor nation. . . . It is the failure to apprehend this great truth that induces so many unsuccessful attempts at final compromise between the slave and the free States; and it is the existence of this great fact that renders all such pretended compromises, when made, vain and ephem-eral."

Finer reading of a national horoscope no statesman ever made ; clearer glance into the dim-lit future has rarely been vouch-

'safed to holy prophet after long vigils of
fasting and prayer at Sinai or Nebo. And
yet what a stunning concert—or rather dis-
sonance of shriek, and yell, and hostile
bray these twin utterances evoked, from ten
thousand groaning stumps, from a thousand
truculent, shrewish journals! An open adhe-
sion to atheism or anarchy could hardly
have called forth fiercer or more scathing
execrations. Yet looking back through an
eventful interval of less than a decade we
see that no truth is more manifest, and
hardly one was at that moment more perti-
nent, than that so clearly yet so inoffen-
sively stated, first by the Western lawyer
and candidate, then by the New York
senator.

I invoke that truth to-day as a bar to
harsh judgments and bitter denunciations—
as a balm to the wounds of the nation.
There *was* "an irrepressible conflict," the
Union *could not* "endure half slave and half
free." The interests of slave-holders and
free labor *were* antagonistic, and it was by
no contrivance of politicians, but in spite of

their determined efforts, that the slavery
question was perpetually, with brief intervals, distracting Congress and involving the
North and the South in fierce collision.
Shallow talkers say, " If it had not been for
this or that—if there had been no Calhoun
or no Garrison, no Wendell Phillips or no
Wise—if John Brown had died ten years
sooner, or Jeff Davis had never been born,
there would have been no Nebraska question ; no secession ; no civil war." Idle,
empty babble, dallying with surfaces and
taking no account of the essential and the
inevitable! If none of the hundred best-
known and most widely hated of our not-
ables of the last twenty years had ever
been born, the late struggle might have
been postponed a few years or might have
been hastened, but it could not have been
averted. It broke out in God's good time
because it had to be—because the elements
of discord embedded in our institutions
could no longer be held passive; it suddenly closed when its divine end had, so
far as war could subserve it, been fully ac-

complished. Such are the convictions which have impelled me to plead for amnesty, and charity, and mercy, and oblivion, as I should have pleaded, though with even less effect, had the other party triumphed. Though there had never been a Missouri to admit, a Texas to annex, nor a Kansas to organize and colonize with free labor or with slave, the " conflict between opposing and enduring forces" would, nevertheless, have wrought out its natural results.

I cannot help regarding that senatorial contest of 1858, between Lincoln and Douglas, as one of the most characteristic and at the same time most creditable incidents in our national history. There was an honest and earnest difference with regard to a most important and imminent public question ; and Illinois was very equally divided thereon, with a United States senator for six years to be chosen by the legislature then to be elected. Hereupon each party selects its ablest and most trusted champion, nominates him for the coveted post, and sends him out as the authorized, indorsed,

accredited champion of its princip.es and
policy to canvass the State and secure a
verdict for its cause. So the two champions
traversed the prairies, speaking alternately
to the same vast audiences at several central, accessible points, and speaking separately at others, until the day of election;
when Douglas secured a small majority in
either branch of the legislature, and was reelected, though Lincoln had the larger popular vote. But while Lincoln had spent less
than a thousand dollars in all, Douglas had
borrowed and disbursed in the canvass no
less than eighty thousand dollars, incurring
a debt which weighed him down to the
grave. I presume no dime of this was used
to buy up his competitor's voters, but all to
organize and draw out his own; still the
debt so improvidently, if not culpably, incurred remained to harass him out of this
mortal life.

Lincoln it was said was beaten: it was a
hasty, erring judgment. This canvass made
him stronger at home, and stronger with the
Republicans of the whole country. And

when the next national convention of his
party assembled, eighteen months thereafter,
he became its nominee for President, and
thus achieved the highest station in the gift
of his countrymen; which but for that misjudged defeat of 1858 he would never have
attained.

A great deal of knowing smartness has
been lavished on that Chicago nomination.
If A had not wanted this, or had B been
satisfied with that, or C not been offended
because he had missed or been refused
something else, the result would have been
different, says Shallowpate. But know, O
Shallowpate! that Lincoln was nominated
for the one sufficient reason that he could
obtain more electoral votes than any of his
competitors! And that reason rarely or
never fails in a national convention. It
nominated Harrison in '39; Polk in '44;
Taylor in '48; Pierce in '52; Buchanan in
'56; and Lincoln in '60. Those who com-
pose national conventions are generally at
least shrewd politicians. They want to secure a triumph if for no better reason than

that they hope thereby to gratify their own personal aspirations. So they consult and compare and balance popularities, and weigh probabilities; and at last the majority centre upon that candidate who can poll most votes. This may not be an exalted test of statesmanship, but it is at least intelligible. And thus Abraham Lincoln became President, having every electoral vote from the free States, but three of the seven cast from New Jersey.

Then followed secession, and confederation, and civil war, whereof the first scenes had been enacted before Mr. Lincoln commenced his journey to Washington, taking leave of his fellow-citizens of Springfield with prophetic tenderness and solemnity, and thenceforward addressing at almost every stopping-place vast crowds who would have speeches, though he would and should have kept silence; and so meandering to the nation's capitol, everywhere cheered and welcomed, though nearly half his auditors had voted against him, until he neared the slave line; and now he was overpersuaded by the

urgent representations of Senator Seward
and General Scott, based upon the espials
and discoveries of Police - Superintendent
Kennedy, to break his engagement to trav-
erse Baltimore, as he had traversed New
York and other cities which had given
heavy majorities against him, and take instead a sleeping car which, passing through
Baltimore in the dead of night, landed him
in Washington hours before that wherein he
was expected publicly to enter Baltimore.

I have no doubt that there was a plot to
assassinate him on his way through Baltimore—that the outbreak which cost the
lives of six Massachusetts volunteers would
have been anticipated by two weeks had he
afforded the opportunity; but this peril of
assassination is one of the inevitable attend-
ants of conspicuous activity in public affairs
in times of popular passion. I cannot say
how many distinct, written notices that *my*
life was forfeited, and the forfeit would soon
be exacted, I have been honored with—certainly a dozen, possibly a hundred; and,
arguing from the little to the great, I have

no doubt that Mr. Lincoln's allotment of these seductive billets must have considerably exceeded ten thousand.

But what then? Must we sit up all night because so many people die in their beds? We cannot evade the assassin; we cannot fence him out, or Henry IV. of France, and ever so many more powerful and beloved monarchs, would not have succumbed to the dagger, the pistol, or the bowl. The most powerful of living rulers is Alexander II. of Russia, and his life has twice within a few years past been saved by the inaccuracy of a regicide's aim. The words of the mighty Julius, as rendered by Shakespeare, embody the truest and highest wisdom:

Cowards die many times before their deaths;
The valiant never taste of death but once.
Of all the wonders that I yet have heard,
It seems to me most strange that men should fear;
Seeing that death, a necessary end,
Will come when it will come.

I am quite certain that this was also Mr. Lincoln's profound conviction, and that he acted on it whenever he was not overruled by a clamor too sudden and too weighty to allow his judgment fair play. "Hence his untimely death," you say. I do not believe it: you may renounce the sunlight and sit trembling in an inner dungeon surrounded by triple walls and triple guards, and yet the assassin will steal in upon you unawares. There is no absolute safeguard against him; your only refuge is the assurance that

Man is immortal 'til his work is done.

Despite ten thousand menaces and warnings and offers to pay for his taking off, and to take him off for pay, Mr. Lincoln was inaugurated President. No crack of rifle or bark of revolver interrupted the reading of his inaugural, though I confidently expected and awaited it. Under a bright March sun, surrounded by a brilliant *cortège* of foreign ministers and home dignitaries, the new President read the inaugural, which he had evidently prepared with care and anxious deliberation before leaving his distant home. That document will be lingered over and

admired long after we shall all have passed
away. It was a masterly effort at persua-
sion and conciliation by one whose command of logic was as perfect as his reliance
on it was unqualified. The man evidently
believed with all his soul that if he could
but convince the South that he would arrest
and return her fugitive slaves, and offered to
slavery every support required by comity or
by the letter of the Constitution, he would
avert her hostility, dissolve the Confederacy,
and restore throughout the Union the sway
of the Federal authority and laws! There
was never a wilder delusion. I doubt
whether one single individual was recalled
from meditated rebellion to loyalty by that
overture; yet mark how solemnly, how tenderly, he pleads in closing it that war may
be averted:

If it were admitted that you who are dissatisfied hold the right side in the dispute,
there is still no single reason for precipitate
action. Intelligence, patriotism, Christianity, and
a firm reliance on Him who has never yet for-

saken this favored land are still competent to adjust, in the best way, all our present difficulties.

In your hands, my dissatisfied fellow-countrymen, and not in mine, is the momentous issue of civil war. The Government will not assail you.

You can have no conflict without being yourselves the aggressors. You can have no oath registered in heaven to destroy the Government ; while I shall have the most solemn one to "preserve, protect, and defend" it.

I am loath to close. We are not enemies, but friends. We must not be enemies. Though passion may have strained, it must not break, our bonds of affection.

The mystic chords of memory, stretching from every battle-field and patriot grave to every living heart and hearthstone all over this broad land, will yet swell the chorus of the Union, when again touched, as surely they will be, by the better angels of our nature.

I apprehend that Mr. Lincoln was very nearly the last man in the country, whether North or South, to relinquish his rooted conviction that the growing chasm might be closed and the Union fully restored without the shedding of blood. Inured to the ways of the Bar and the Stump, so long accustomed to hear of rebellions that never came to light, he long and obstinately refused to believe that reason and argument, fairly employed, could fail of their proper effect. Though Montgomery Blair, that member of his cabinet who best understood the Southern character, strenuously insisted from the outset that war was inevitable, that hard knocks must be given and taken before the authority of the Union could be restored or would be recognized in the Cotton States, the President gave far greater heed to the counsel and anticipations of his Secretary of State, whose hopeful nature and optimistic views were in accordance with his own stubborn prepossessions.

I saw him for a short hour about a fortnight after his inauguration; and though the tidings of General Twiggs's treacherous surrender of the larger portion of our little

army, hitherto employed in guarding our
Mexican frontier, had been some days at
hand, I saw and heard nothing that indicated or threatened belligerency on our
part. On the contrary, the President sat
listening to the endless whine of office-seek-
ers, and doling out village post-offices to
importunate or lucky partisans, just as
though we were sailing before land breezes
on a smiling, summer sea; and to my inquiry, "Mr. President, do you know that
you will have to *fight* for the place in
which you sit?" he answered pleasantly—I
will not say lightly—but in words which intimated his disbelief that any fighting would
transpire or be needed: and I firmly believe
that this dogged resolution not to believe
that our country was about to be drenched
in fraternal blood is the solution of his
obstinate tameness throughout the earlier
stages of the war; and especially his patient
listening to the demand of a deputation
from the Young Christians of Baltimore, as
well as of the mayor and of other civic dignitaries, that he should stipulate while block-

aded in Washington, and in imminent danger of capture or expulsion, that no more
Northern volunteers should cross the sacred
soil of Maryland in hastening to his relief.
We could not comprehend this at the North
—many of us have not yet seen through it:
most certainly if he had required a committee of ten thousand to kick the bearers of
this preposterously impudent demand back
to Baltimore, the ranks of that committee
could have been filled in an hour from any
Northern city or county containing fifty
thousand inhabitants.

And thus the precious early days of the
conflict were surrendered because the President did not even yet believe that any serious conflict would be had. He still clung
to the delusion that forbearance, and pa-
tience, and moderation, and soft words
would yet obviate all necessity for deadly
strife. Thus new volunteers were left for
weeks to rot in idleness and dissipation in
the outskirts and purlieus of Washington,
because their commander-in-chief believed
that it would never be necessary or advis-

able to load their muskets with ball-cartridges. But when at length that heartless, halting, desolating, stumbling, staggering, fatally delayed advance to Bull Run was made by half the regiments that should have been sent forward, and had recoiled in ignominious disaster, as an advance so made against a compact, determined, decently handled force always must, there came a decided change. The wanton rout of that black day cost the President but one night's sleep. It cost me a dozen while good men died of it who had never been within two hundred miles of the so quickly deserted field. Henceforth Mr. Lincoln accepted war as a stern necessity, and stood ready to fight it out to the bitter end.

And yet while I judge that many were more eager than he to bring the struggle to an early if worthy close, no one would have welcomed an honorable and lasting pacification with a sincerer joy. No man was ever more grossly misrepresented or more widely misapprehended than he was on this point; and I deem the fault partly his own or that of his immediate counsellors. Let me state distinctly how and why.

The Rebellion, once fairly inaugurated, was kept alive and aggravated by systematic and monstrous misrepresentation at the South of the spirit and purposes of the North. That our soldiers were sent down to kill, ravage, and destroy, with " Beauty and Booty" on their standards, and rage and lust in their hearts; and that the North would be satisfied with nothing less than the utter spoliation, if not the absolute extirpation, of the Southern people—such were the tales currently reported and widely believed in that vast region wherein no journal not avowedly Confederate existed or could exist for years. Much of the strength of the Rebellion lay in a widespread belief within its domain that nothing worse could possibly happen to its adherents or their families than subjugation to the Union. Hence I hold that our Government, whatever its hopes of a favorable issue, should not only have welcomed every overture looking to pacification from the other side, but should have studied and

planned to multiply opportunities for con-
ference and negotiation. When Henry May,
an anti-war representative of Baltimore, in
Congress, sought permission to go to Richmond in quest of peace, Mr. Lincoln allowed him to slip clandestinely through our
lines, but kept his mission quiet and dis-
claimed all responsibility for it. I would
have publicly said: "Go in welcome, Mr.
May: I only stipulate that you publish, and
authenticate by your signature, the very
best terms that are offered you at Richmond; and I agree if they be responsibly
indorsed to give them a prompt, unpreju-
diced consideration." And I would have
repeated this to every Democrat who might
at any time have solicited like permission.
So, when in July, 1863, Mr. A. H. Stephens
sought permission to visit Washington in a
Confederate gunboat with some sort of overture, I would have responded: "Spare us
your gunboat, Mr. S.,—that would be super-
fluous here; but you will find a swift vessel
and a safe-conduct awaiting you at Fortress
Monroe: so come to us at once, -properly

accredited, and you will find us not merely willing, but anxious, to stay this revolting effusion of human blood." And so to the last. I do firmly believe that the President's Niagara card, "To whom it may Concern," did much to disabuse the Southern mind with regard to Northern purposes, and might have been so framed and proffered as to have done very much more. Had it said directly, affirmatively, what it said inferentially, negatively, I believe it would have paralyzed thousands of arms then striking frenziedly at the best of their and our country. And I hold Mr. Lincoln's ultimate visit to Fortress Monroe, there to confer with Stephens, Hunter, and Campbell, with a view to peace, one of the wisest and noblest acts of an eventful, illustrious life, and one which contributed more than many a Union victory to the speedy disintegration and collapse of the Rebellion. Honored be the wisdom that comes late, if it be not indeed *too* late!

As to the slavery question, I think Mr. Lincoln resolutely looked away from it so

long as he could, because he feared that
his recognizing slavery as the mainspring
and driving-wheel of the Rebellion was calculated to weaken the Union cause by de-
taching Maryland, Kentucky, and possibly
Missouri also, from its support. "One war
at a time" was his wise veto on any
avoidable foreign complication; and in the
same spirit he vetoed Fremont's and
Phelps's, and Hunter's, and other early
efforts to liberate the slaves of rebels, or to
enlist negro troops. I am not arguing that
he was right or wrong in any particular instance: I am only setting forth his way of
looking at these grave questions, and the
point of view from which he regarded them.
To deal with each question as it arose and
not be embarrassed in so dealing with it by
preconceptions and premature committals,
and never to widen needlessly the circle of
our enemies, was his inflexible rule. Hence
when Congress, in the summer of 1864,
named and enacted an elaborate plan of
reconstruction for the States then in revolt
—which bill was presented to him during

the last hour of the session—he withheld his signature and thereby caused its failure —not, as he explained, that he was adverse to the conditions proposed therein, but that he "refused to be inflexibly committed to *any* single plan of restoration" while the Rebellion was still unsubdued, and while exigencies might arise in the progress of the conflict, which could not be foreseen. The document wherein Messrs. Wade and Winter Davis criticised and controverted this decision is far clearer and more caustic than any Mr. Lincoln ever wrote; and yet I believe the judgment of posterity will be that he had the right side of the question.

I am not so clear that he had the better position in his discussion with Messrs. Corning and other Democrats of Albany, and in his like correspondence with Democratic leaders in Ohio touching the arrest and punishment of Mr. Vallandigham. The essential question at issue was this: " How far may a citizen lawfully and with impunity oppose a war which his country is waging?" It is a question as old as human freedom, and its

settlement has not yet been approximated.
That there must be liberty to nominate and
support candidates hostile to the further
prosecution of the contest, and in favor of
decisive efforts looking to its speedy close
by negotiation, is not contested ; but where
is the limit of this liberty? May the Opposition proceed to arraign the President as
a usurper, despot, anarchist, murderer, and
eulogize the cause of the public enemy as
righteous, patriotic, and entitled to every
good man's sympathy and support? If not,
where is the freedom of discussion in election? If yea, how is the national authority
to be upheld and its right in extremity to
the best services of the whole people en-
forced and maintained? Mr. Vallandigham
was and had been an open, unqualified, consistent opponent of the War for the Union.
He held that war to be unjust, unconstitutional, and wantonly aggressive. He held
that the Union could only be restored
through the discomfiture of the national
forces and the consequent abandonment of
all attempts to "coerce" the South. There

was nothing equivocal in his attitude, nor in
his utterances, whether in Congress or on
the stump. And it cannot be fairly denied
that his speeches were as clearly giving " aid
and comfort" to the enemy as were the
cavalry raids of John Morgan, J. E. B.
Stuart, or Mosby. So General Burnside,
commanding the military department including Ohio, had him arrested, tried by a
court-martial, convicted, and sentenced to
imprisonment in a fortress; which sentence
was commuted by the President into banishment to the Southern Confederacy—which
sentence was duly executed. And thereupon
Mr. V—— was nominated for Governor by
the Democracy of Ohio, and a strong appeal
made to the President by the Democrats of
Albany and elsewhere for an unconditional
reversal of the sentence of banishment, as-
suming that Mr. V—— had been condemned
and banished in violation of law and right
—" for no other reason than words addressed
to a public meeting in criticism of the
course of the administration, and in con-
demnation of the military orders of " Burn-

side. I think Mr. V——'s friends have
ground to stand upon so strong—or at least
so plausible—that they might well have
offered to set forth more broadly and fairly
the position and the action they controverted.

Mr. Lincoln answered them in what I consider the most masterly document that ever
came from his pen. I doubt that Webster
could have done better—I am sure he could
not have so clearly and so forcibly appealed
to the average comprehension of his countrymen: it is clear enough from his letter
that the whole business was distasteful to
him—that he thought Burnside had blun-
dered in meddling at all with Vallandigham,
or even recognizing his existence. Indeed,
he intimates this quite plainly in the course
of his letter; yet he braces himself for his
task, and fully justifies therein the claim I
set up for him, that he was the cleverest
logician for the masses that America has yet
produced. Six years before he had crushed
by a sentence the sophism that sought to
cover the extension of slavery into the Ter-

ritories with the mantle of "Popular Sov-
ereignty:" "It means," said he, "that if A
chooses to make B his slave, C shall not interfere to prevent him." So, in answering
Messrs. Corning and Co., he treated their
letter as covering a demand that the rebel
cause might be served and promoted in the
loyal States with impunity by any action
that would not be unlawful in times of profound peace—a position that he stoutly contested. He says of the Albany proposition:

The resolutions promise to support me in
every constitutional and lawful measure to suppress the Rebellion; and I have not knowingly
employed, nor shall knowingly employ, any
other. But the meeting, by their resolutions,
assert and argue that certain military arrests,
and proceedings following them, for which I am
ultimately responsible, are unconstitutional. I
think they are not. The resolutions quote from
the Constitution the definition of treason, and
also the limiting safeguards and guarantees
therein provided for the citizen on trial for
treason, and on his being held to answer for
capital or otherwise infamous crimes, and in

criminal prosecutions, his right to a speedy and public trial by an impartial jury. They proceed to resolve "that these safeguards of the rights of the citizen against the pretensions of arbitrary power were intended more *especially* for his protection in times of civil commotion." And, apparently to demonstrate the proposition, the resolutions proceed: "They were secured substantially to the English people *after* years of protracted civil war, and were adopted into our Constitution at the *close* of the Revolution." Would not the demonstration have been better if it could have been truly said that these safeguards had been adopted and applied *during* the civil wars, and *during* our Revolution, instead of *after* the one and at the *close* of the other? I, too, am devotedly for them *after* civil war, and *before* civil war, and at all times, "except when, in cases of rebellion or invasion, the public safety may require their suspension." The resolutions proceed to tell us that these safeguards "have stood the test of seventy-six years of trial, under our republican system, under circumstances which show that, while they constitute the foundation of all free government, they are elements of the enduring sta-

bility of the Republic." No one denies that
they have so stood the test up to the beginning
of the present Rebellion, if we except a certain
occurrence at New Orleans; nor does any one
question that they will stand the same test
much longer after the Rebellion closes.

Further on he says:

. . . He who dissuades one man from volun-
teering, or induces one soldier to desert, weak-
ens the Union cause as much as he who kills a
Union soldier in battle. Yet this dissuasion or
inducement may be so conducted as to be no
defined crime of which any civil court would
take cognizance.

And still further on:

Of how little value the constitutional provis-
ions I have quoted will be rendered, if arrests
shall never be made until defined crimes shall
have been committed, may be illustrated by a
few notable examples. Gen. John C. Breckin-
ridge, Gen. Robert E. Lee, Gen. Joseph E.
Johnston, Gen. John B. Magruder, Gen. William
Preston, Gen. Simon B. Buckner, and Commo-

dore Franklin Buchanan, now occupying the
very highest places in the Rebel war service,
were all within the power of the Government
since the Rebellion began, and were nearly as
well known to be traitors then as now. Unquestionably, if we had seized them and held
them, the insurgent cause would be much
weaker. But no one of them had then committed any crime defined in the law. Every
one of them, if arrested, would have been discharged on *habeas corpus* were the writ allowed
to operate. In view of these and similar cases,
I think the time not unlikely to come when I
shall be blamed for having made too few arrests
rather than too many.

At length near the close of his letter, he
sums up the case in his masterly strain of
argumentation:

I understand the meeting, whose resolutions
I am considering, to be in favor of suppressing
the Rebellion by military force—by armies.
Long experience has shown that armies cannot
be maintained unless desertions shall be pun-
ished by the severe penalty of death. The case
requires, and the law and the Constitution sanc-

tion, this punishment. Must I shoot a simple-minded soldier boy who deserts, while I must not touch a hair of a wily agitator who induces him to desert? This is none the less injurious when effected by getting a father, a brother, or friend into a public meeting, and there working upon his feelings till he is persuaded to write the soldier boy that he is fighting in a bad cause, for a wicked Administration of a contemptible Government, too weak to arrest and punish him if he shall desert. I think that, in such a case, to silence the agitator and save the boy is not only constitutional but withal a great mercy.

If I be wrong on this question of constitutional power, my error lies in believing that certain proceedings are constitutional when, in cases of rebellion or invasion, the public safety requires them, which would not be constitutional when, in the absence of rebellion or invasion, the public safety does *not* require them; in other words, that the Constitution is not, in its application, in all respects the same, in cases of rebellion or invasion involving the public safety, as it is in times of profound peace and public security. The Constitution itself makes the dis-

tinction; and I can no more be persuaded that
the Government can constitutionally take no
strong measures in time of rebellion, because it
can be shown that the same could not be lawfully taken in time of peace, than I could be
persuaded that a particular drug is not good
medicine for a sick man because it can be
shown not to be good food for a well one.
Nor am I able to appreciate the danger appre-
hended by the meeting, that the American people will, by means of military arrests during the
Rebellion, lose sight of public discussion, the
liberty of speech and the press, the law of evidence, trial by jury, and *habeas corpus*, throughout the indefinite peaceful future, which I trust
lies before them, any more than I am able to
believe that a man could contract so strong an
appetite for emetics during a temporary illness
as to persist in feeding upon them during the
remainder of his healthful life.

I do not suppose this logic convinced Mr.
Lincoln that the arrest and trial and conviction of Mr. V—— were wise and useful
measures of repression—if it did, it has had
no kindred effect on *my* mind. Yet I hold

that the bitterest opponent of the President and his policy must in fairness admit that the case is not entirely one-sided—that if government is to exist it must have power to suppress rebellion against its authority; and that it is neither reasonable nor possible to accord the same immunities and uniformly respect the same safeguards of free speech and personal liberty in the presence of a gigantic rebellion as in times of public tranquillity and unbroken allegiance to order and law.

I have said that Mr. Lincoln, when I first knew him, was classed with the more conservative of Northern Whigs on the subject of slavery. On the 3d of March, 1837—the last day of General Jackson's rule—he submitted to the Legislature of Illinois a protest against certain pro-slavery resolves passed by the Democratic majority of that body, wherein on behalf of himself and his brethren he says :

They believe that the institution of slavery is founded on both injustice and bad policy, but

that the promulgation of abolition doctrines
tends rather to increase than abate its evils.

They believe that the Congress of the United
States has no power under the Constitution to
interfere with the institution of slavery in the
different States.

They believe that the Congress of the United
States has the power, under the Constitution, to
abolish slavery in the District of Columbia, but
that the power ought not to be exercised, unless
at the request of the people of the District.

In 1848 he voted in Congress (as we have
seen) to lay on the table Mr. Galt's resolve
proposing instructions to the Federal District
Committee to report a bill abolishing slavery
in said district, but submitted a substitute
looking to compensated, gradual emancipation, upon the express assent of a majority
of the legal voters thereof. Ten years later,
instructed by the Nebraska developments he
had advanced, as we have seen, to the con-
ception that "the Union could not permanently endure half slave and half free"—and
that slavery, not the Union, would eventually
have to succumb and disappear. This was a

great stride ; and he had hardly moved again
when he wrote me on the 22d of August,
1862, in reply to an appeal from the pro-
slavery policy which had thus far governed
the practical conduct of the war, this expo-
sition of his war policy :

I would save the Union. I would save it the
shortest way under the Constitution. The
sooner the national authority can be restored,
the nearer the Union will be "the Union as it
was." If there be those who would not save
the Union unless they could at the same time
save slavery, I do not agree with them. If
there be those who would not save the Union
unless they could at the same time *destroy* slavery, I do not agree with them. My paramount
object in this struggle is to save the Union, and
is not either to save or to destroy slavery. If I
could save the Union without freeing any slave,
I would do it; and if I could save it by freeing
all the slaves I would do it; and if I could
save it by freeing some and leaving others
alone, I would also do that. What I do about
slavery and the colored race, I do because I believe it helps to save the Union; and what I

forbear, I forbear because I do not believe it
would help to save the Union. I shall do less
whenever I shall believe what I am doing hurts
the cause, and I shall do more whenever I shall
believe doing more will help the cause. I shall
try to correct errors when shown to be errors,
and I shall adopt new views so fast as they
shall appear to be true views. I have here
stated my purpose according to my view of official duty; and I intend no modification of my
oft-expressed personal wish, that all men everywhere could be free.

Yours,   A. LINCOLN.

This manifesto was exultingly hailed by
the less radical portion of his supporters—I
never could imagine why. It recognized the
right to destroy slavery whenever that step
should be deemed necessary to the national
salvation—nay, it affirmed the *duty* of de-
stroying it in such contingency. And it
proved that the President was meditating
that grave step and clearly perceiving that it
might—nay, probably *would*—become necessary, and that he wished to prepare the public mind for acquiescence therein whenever

he should realize and announce that the time had come. I do not see how these points can have escaped the attention of any acute and careful observer.

It may well be noted here that this letter, though in form a response to my "Prayer of Twenty Millions," was not so in fact; I had not besought him to proclaim general emancipation. I had only urged him to give full effect to the laws of the land, which prescribed that slaves employed with their masters' acquiescence in support of the Rebellion should thenceforth be treated as freed by such employment, and by the general hostility of their owners to the national authority. I have no doubt that Mr. Lincoln's letter had been prepared before he ever saw my "Prayer," and that this was merely used by him as an opportunity, an occasion, an excuse, for setting his own altered position—changed not by his volition, but by circumstances—fairly before the country.

At the same time, I have no doubt that his letter expresses the exact literal truth, precisely as it lay in his mind. Assailed on the one hand as intent on upholding and preserving, on the other as subtly scheming and contriving to subvert and abolish slavery, he was really and truly obnoxious to neither of these charges, but solely, engrossingly intent on putting down the Rebellion, and preserving the Union by any and every means, and ready either to guarantee the perpetuity or proclaim the overthrow of human bondage, according as the one step or the other should seem likely to subserve and secure that end. Hence the first proclamation of freedom, which was issued but a few weeks after the appearance of this letter, seemed to me but the fulfilment of a promise implied in its forerunner.

I did not see the President between the issue of his first and that of his second Proclamation of Freedom—in fact, not from January, 1862, till about February 1, 1863. He then spoke of the Emancipation policy as not having yet effected so much good here at home as had been promised or predicted, but added that it had helped us decidedly in our foreign relations. He intimated no regret that it had been adopted, and, I presume, never felt any. In fact, as he was habitually and constitutionally cautious as to making advances, he seldom or never felt impelled or required to take a step backward. Never putting down his foot till he felt sure there was firm ground beneath it, he never feared to bear his whole weight on it when once fairly down. And, having committed himself to the policy of Emancipation, he proclaimed and justified it in letters to sympathizing British workmen, and to friends and foes on every side. His proposal of gradual and compensated Emancipation in the loyal slave States and districts, his postponed but hearty sanction of the enlistment of Black soldiers, and his persistent and thorough recognition and assertion of the Inalienable Rights of Man, were links in one chain which he wove skilfully, if not nimbly, around the writhing form of the overmastered and panting Rebellion. I am no admirer of the style of his more elaborate and pretentious state papers, especially his messages to Congress. They

lack the fire and force that an Andrew, a
Chase, or even a Stanton would have given
them; they are not electric—not calculated
to touch the chords of the national heart,
and thrill them with patriotic ardor; yet I
doubt that our national literature contains a
finer gem than that little speech at the Get-
tysburg celebration, November 19th, 1863,
wherein, after the close of Mr. Everett's
classic but frigid oration, the President arose
and simply said:

Fourscore and seven years ago our fathers
brought forth upon this continent a new nation,
conceived in liberty, and dedicated to the proposition that all men are created equal.

Now we are engaged in a great civil war,
testing whether that nation, or any other nation
so conceived and so dedicated, can long endure.
We are met on a great battlefield of that war.
We are met to dedicate a portion of it as the
final resting-place of those who here gave their
lives that that nation might live. It is altogether fitting and proper that we should do this.

But in a larger sense, we cannot dedicate—
we cannot consecrate—we cannot hallow this

ground. The brave men, living and dead, who struggled here, have consecrated it far above our power to add or detract. The world will little note, nor long remember what we *say* here, but it can never forget what they *did* here. It is for us, the living, rather to be dedicated here to the unfinished work that they have thus far so nobly carried on. It is rather for us to be here dedicated to the great task remaining before us, that from these honored dead we take increased devotion to the cause for which they here gave the last full measure of devotion, that we here highly resolve that the dead shall not have died in vain; that the nation shall, under God, have a new birth of freedom; and that government of the people, by the people, and for the people shall not perish from the earth.

One more citation, and what seems to me the essential characteristics of the man as truly, unconsciously portrayed in his own acts and words, will have been set fairly before you:

Kentucky had been a chief obstacle to the early adoption of an Emancipation policy. As the President's native State, as the most

central and weighty of the so-called border
States, and as preponderantly favorable to
the Union, though very largely represented
in the rebel armies, the President had long
hesitated and yielded to his natural reluc-
tance to offend her loyal whites, as it was
clear that any act looking to general Emancipation would surely do.

When the die had at length been cast,
and the attitude of the government had become unequivocal, her governor, Bramlett,
with ex-Senator Dickson and Editor A. G.
Hodges, appeared in Washington as bearers
of her solemn protest against that policy.
The President met them cordially, and they
discussed their difference freely and amicably, but neither party seems to have made
much headway in convincing and converting
the other.   After the Kentuckians had left,
Mr. Hodges asked the President to give in
writing the substance of the views he had
set forth during their interview, and he did
it in a letter of remarkable terseness and co-
gency even for him.   I will cite but two
passages which illustrate phases of Mr. Lin-

coln's character and his mode of viewing the great questions at issue, which I have not yet clearly presented. In the former he says:

I am naturally antislavery. If slavery is not wrong, nothing is wrong. I cannot remember when I did not so think and feel. And yet, I have never understood that the Presidency conferred upon me an unrestricted right to act officially upon this judgment and feeling. It was in the oath I took, that I would to the best of my ability preserve, protect, and defend the Constitution of the United States. I could not take the office without taking the oath. Nor was it my view that I might take an oath to get power, and break the oath in using the power. I understood, too, that in ordinary civil administration this oath even forbade. me to practically indulge my primary, abstract judgment on the moral question of slavery. I had publicly declared this many times and in many ways. And I aver that, to this day, I have done no official act in mere deference to my abstract judgment and feeling on slavery.

I did understand, however, that my oath to

preserve the Constitution to the best of my ability imposed upon me the duty of preserving, by every indispensable means, that government —that nation of which that Constitution was the organic law. Was it possible to lose the nation, and yet preserve the Constitution?

By general law, life and limb must be protected ; yet often a limb must be amputated to save a life ; but a life is never wisely given to save a limb. I felt that measures otherwise unconstitutional might become lawful by becoming indispensable to the preservation of the Constitution through the preservation of the nation. Right or wrong, I assume this ground, and now avow it. I could not feel that, to the best of my ability, I had even tried to preserve the Constitution, if, to save slavery or any minor matter, I should permit the wreck of the government, country, and Constitution, all together

Having briefly set forth how and why he was driven by the difficulty of subduing the Rebellion first to proclaim Emancipation, and then to summon blacks as well as whites to the defence of the country, and

barely glancing at the advantages thus secured, he closes with these words :

And now let any Union man who complains
of the measure test himself by writing down in
one line that he is for subduing the Rebellion
by force of arms, and in the next that he is
for taking these hundred and thirty thousand
men from the Union side, and placing them
where they would be but for the measure he
condemns. If he cannot face his case so
stated, it is only because he cannot face the
truth.

I add a word which was not in the verbal
conversation. In telling this tale I attempt no
compliment to my own sagacity. I claim not
to have controlled events, but confess plainly
that events have controlled me. Now, at the
end of three years' struggle, the nation's condition is not what either party or any man de-
vised or expected : God alone can claim it.
Whither it is tending seems plain. If God now
wills the removal of a great wrong, and wills
also that we of the North as well as you of the
South shall pay fairly for our complicity in
that wrong, impartial history will find therein

new cause to attest and revere the justice and
goodness of God.

Yours truly,

A. LINCOLN.

Those few words: " I attempt no compliment to my own sagacity. I claim not to
have controlled events, but confess plainly
that events have controlled me," furnish a
key to the whole character and career of
the man. He was no inspired Elijah or
John Baptist, emerging from the awful desert sanctified by lonely fastings and wrest-
lings with Satan in prayer, to thrill adoring,
suppliant multitudes with unwonted fires of
penitence and devotion; he was no royal
singer of Israel, touching at will his harp
and sweeping all the chords of emotion and
aspiration in the general heart: he was
simply a plain, true, earnest, patriotic man,
gifted with eminent common-sense, which
in its wide range gave a hand to shrewd-
ness on the one hand, humor on the other,
and which allied him intimately, warmly,
with the masses of mankind. I doubt

whether man, woman, or child, white or black, bond or free, virtuous or vicious, ever accosted or reached forth a hand to Abraham Lincoln, and detected in his countenance or manner any repugnance or shrinking from the proffered contact, any assumption of superiority or betrayal of disdain. No one was ever more steeped in the spirit of that glorious lyric of the inspired Scotch ploughman—

A man 's a man, for a' that ;

and no one was ever acquainted and on terms of friendly intimacy with a greater number of human beings of all ranks and conditions than was he whom the bullet of Wilkes Booth claimed for its victim.

I pass over his reëlection, his second inaugural, his final visit to the army of the Potomac, and his entry into Richmond, hard on the heels of its long-postponed capture ; I say nothing of his manifest determination to treat the prostrate insurgents with unexampled magnanimity, and the terrible crime which with singular madness quenched, under the impulse of intense sympathy with the Rebellion, the life which was at that moment of greater importance and value to the rebels than that of any other living man. All these have added nothing to the symmetry of a character which was already rounded and complete. Never before did one so constantly and visibly *grow* under the discipline of incessant cares, anxieties, and trials. The Lincoln of '62 was plainly a larger, broader, better man than he had been in '61 ; while '63 and '64 worked his continued and unabated growth in mental and moral stature. Few have been more receptive, more sympathetic, and (within reasonable limits) more plastic than he. Had he lived twenty years longer, I believe he would have steadily increased in ability to counsel his countrymen, and in the estimation of the wise and good.

But he could in no case have lived so long. "Perfect through suffering" is the divine law; and the tension of mind and body through his four years of eventful rule had told fearfully upon his physical frame. When I last saw him, some five or six weeks before his death, his face was haggard with care, and seamed with thought and trouble. It looked care-ploughed, tempest-tossed, weather-beaten, as if he were some tough old mariner, who had for years been beating up against wind and tide, unable to make his port or find safe anchorage. Judging from that scathed, rugged countenance, I do not believe he could have lived out his second term had no felon hand been lifted against his priceless life.

The chief moral I deduce from his eventful career asserts

The might that slumbers in a peasant's arm !

the majestic heritage, the measureless opportunity, of the humblest American youth. Here was an heir of poverty and insignificance, obscure, untaught, buried throughout his childhood in the frontier forests, with no transcendent, dazzling abilities, such as make their way in any country, under any institu-

tions, but emphatically in intellect, as in station, one of the millions of strivers for a
rude livelihood, who, though attaching himself stubbornly to the less popular party,
and especially so in the State which he had
chosen as his home, did nevertheless become
a central figure of the Western Hemisphere,
and an object of honor, love, and reverence
throughout the civilized world. Had he
been a genius, an intellectual prodigy, like
Julius Cæsar, or Shakspere, or Mirabeau, or
Webster, we might say: " This lesson is not
for us—with such faculties any one could
achieve and succeed;" but he was not a
born king of men, ruling by the resistless
might of his natural superiority, but a child
of the people, who made himself a great
persuader, therefore a leader, by dint of firm
resolve, and patient effort, and dogged per-
severance. He slowly won his way to emi-
nence and renown by ever doing the work
that lay next to him—doing it with all his
growing might—doing it as well as he
could, and learning by his failure, when failure was encountered, how to do it better.

Wendell Phillips once coarsely said, "He grew because we watered him;" which was only true in so far as this—he was open to all impressions and influences, and gladly profited by all the teachings of events and circumstances, no matter how adverse or un-welcome. There was probably no year of his life in which he was not a wiser, larger, better man than he had been the year pre-ceding. It was of such a nature—patient, plodding, sometimes groping, but ever towards the light—that Tennyson sings:

Perplext in faith, but pure in deeds,
　At last he beat his music out.
　There lives more faith in honest doubt,
Believe me, than in half the creeds.

There are those who profess to have been always satisfied with his conduct of the war, deeming it prompt, energetic, vigorous, mas-terly. I did not, and could not, so regard it. I believed then—I believe this hour—that a Napoleon I., a Jackson, would have crushed secession out in a single short cam-

paign—almost in a single victory. I believed
that an advance to Richmond 100,000 strong
might have been made by the end of June,
1861 ; that would have insured a counter-
revolution throughout the South, and a vol-
untary return of every State, through a dis-
persion and disavowal of its rebel chiefs,
to the councils and the flag of the Union.
But such a return would have not merely
left slavery intact—it would have established
it on firmer foundations than ever before.
The momentarily alienated North and South
would have fallen on each other's necks,
and, amid tears and kisses, have sealed their
reunion by ignominiously making the Black
the scapegoat of their bygone quarrel, and
wreaking on him the spite which they had
purposed to expend on each other. But
God had higher ends, to which a Bull Run,
a Ball's Bluff, a Gaines's Mill, a Groveton,
were indispensable: and so they came to
pass, and were endured and profited by.
The Republic needed to be passed through
chastening, purifying fires of adversity and
suffering: so these came and did their work

and the verdure of a new national life springs greenly, luxuriantly, from their ashes. Other men were helpful to the great renovation, and nobly did their part in it ; yet, looking back through the lifting mists of seven eventful, tragic, trying, glorious years, I clearly discern that the one providential leader, the indispensable hero of the great drama—faithfully reflecting even in his hesitations and seeming vacillations the sentiment of the masses—fitted by his very defects and shortcomings for the burden laid upon him, the good to be wrought out through him, was Abraham Lincoln.

LETTERS TO
CHARLES A. DANA.

PREFACE TO THE DANA LETTERS.

THE following letters, which Mr. Dana has put unreservedly in my hands for this volume, touch a very interesting period of *ante-bellum* history. But they do more than merely relate to the protracted struggle over the election of a Speaker for the Thirty-fourth Congress. As Mr. Dana has said, "incidentally they discuss a great many other topics; and the wit, the humor, and the originality of every line will be sure to arrest the attention of the reader." The special references in them to the conduct of the *Tribune* thirty-seven years ago are not only interesting to the lay reader, but will prove specially attractive to the newspaper manager of to-day.

How swiftly history moves, one may see, as Mr. Dana remarks, by the names which are emphasized in these letters. Some of them are not now of much account; a few, like those of Seward, Chase, Benton, and Clayton, are still remembered. But of Mr. Lincoln, Jefferson Davis, John Sherman, Stanton, Andrew, Grant, McClellan, and other great generals and civilians—all famous ten years after these letters were written—almost nothing is here foreshadowed.

It is not easy to edit by expurgation letters so freely expressed as these; and they are therefore left exactly as they were written, with only a few names omitted. It is believed that nothing which remains in them as personal reference will now offend the living or harm the dead.

The letters here produced are all that are left of those written by Mr. Greeley to Mr. Dana. Many others were once in existence, but before their value became impressive they were, at different times, lost or destroyed.

Mr. Dana's comment upon Mr. Greeley is

perhaps a fit conclusion to what needs saying about this particular correspondence:

" Mr. Greeley's first thought was always
for the *Tribune*, and this was the case with
him to the end of his career. And what a
noble and useful career it was! Even the
final failure, and the tragic end which disappointment brought upon him, contained
nothing foolish or ignoble. Indeed, it was
nothing worse than failure; and this has
not been thought to involve any special con-
demnation in the case of others who, like
him, have had to figure before the public as
defeated candidates. And we must add, too,
that none of these or any other kind of citi-
zens has ever exceeded him in virtue, in
fidelity to the principles of freedom and
progress, in unswerving devotion to the republic, or in love for that great unity of
humanity in which every individual is but a
fragment, an atom seen for the passing
hour, and living and acting but to disappear
at last."

J. B.

LETTERS TO CHARLES A. DANA.

WASHINGTON, D. C., Dec. 1, 1855.

FRIEND DANA: I think ——— worth $150 per month. He has facilities at the west end which I have not and never can have, and living here is horribly dear for those who have to see people. By and by he may perfect his opportunities with Marcy & Co., and then you can stop him. For the present better pay $200 a month than lose him. I see him and confer with him several times a day; but it is best that the business should all go through one channel. So I wish you would write him accepting his terms. If you can easily repeat the hint I have given him, that we value facts more than opinions, it will be well. Everybody we employ to gather information seems to

think he has the paper to edit, and I expect soon to have a notice from Dennis
that, if we don't change our course on some
public question, he will be obliged to relieve
himself of all responsibility in the premises
by dissolving his connection with the *Tribune*.

I thank you for your reply to Dr. Bailey.
He is eaten up with the idea of making
Chase President.

I am doing what I can for Banks; but
he won't be Speaker. His support of the
Republicans against the K. N. ticket this
fall renders it impossible. If we elect anybody it will be Pennington or Fuller. I
fear the latter. Pennington is pretty fair,
considering. He will try to twist himself
into the proper shape, but I would greatly
prefer one who had the natural crook.

Phelps to-night announced in Democratic
caucus that two of the Missouri Whigs
would vote their side. Glad of it.

The news from Kansas is helping us.

You ought to see the loving glances I
get from Whitfield. We know each other

first-rate, but are not introduced. I think the House will organize on Monday; if not, Tuesday will fetch it.

I hate this hole, but am glad I have come. It does me good to see how those who hate the *Tribune* much, fear it yet more. There are a dozen here who will do better for my eye being on them. Schouler is particularly cordial.

As to old McRea, I think, we may as well let him have his $10 a week for a few weeks yet, though I can't use him. I wouldn't mind his being a genius, if he was not a fool. He has no idea of keeping his mouth shut, but tells everybody he is connected with the *Tribune,* but doesn't go its isms, etc. He annoys me to the amount of $10 per week at least; but let him wait a little. Yours, H. G.

C. A. DANA, Esq.

II.

WASHINGTON, Jan. 7, 1856.

FRIEND DANA: What would it cost to burn the Opera House? If the price is reasonable, have it done and send me the bill.

I think this last is the most unlucky week the *Tribune* ever saw — beaten in the documents and beaten every way beside.

It is unaccountable to me that Hildreth did not review the Pro-Slavery part of the message in three or four crisp editorials of a column each. It *belonged* to the *Tribune* to do that, and the whole country expected it of us. It was a great mistake to neglect our proper work and undertake instead the unpopular and unplausible defence of the British side of the Nicaragua question. We have lost ground terribly by this, and must try to regain it somehow. All Congress is disappointed and grieved at not seeing Pierce and Cushing demolished in the *Tribune*. I wrote my two letters under the presumption (there being no paper on Wednesday) that the solid work of exposing their perversions of history had, of course, been done by Hildreth. I should have dealt with it even more gravely but for that. And now I see (the Saturday's paper only got through last night) that you have crowded out what little I *did* send to make room for Fry's eleven columns of arguments as to the feasibility of sustaining the opera in N. Y., if they would only play his compositions. I don't believe three hundred people who take the *Tribune* care one chew of tobacco for the matter. I am very sorry that we can't discuss such a message *somehow* in the week of its issue.

Now as to documents. Harvey went to the Department on Thursday for the Treasury report, as he had been advised beforehand that it would then be ready for him, and was now told by Peter Washington that *he had let some copies go off by that morning's mail.* Of course, being told that he was anticipated, he did not suppose that sending the great budget now was of any consequence. Was not this a reasonable conclusion? I admit that he should have got two copies and sent one on to you; but he got only one, and left that at my room, and I only found it when I came down from the House, too late to

send by that evening's mail; so I did all
I could do—extracted some of the most
pregnant passages and sent them to you in
a letter discussing them. Since you did not
find room even for these, I infer that more
could hardly have fared better.

I began this letter to apologize for taking
up three or four columns with a controversy
with Dick Thompson, which I shall send
you to-day probably by Adam's Express.
Considering, however, those XIX columns of
Coroner Fry's inquest on the putrefying
opera, I *won't* apologize. This controversy
concerns not Dick Thompson only, but the
whole breed of Whig Doughfaces, and the
room is well spent. You must give it soon
—on the outside, of course. Yours, sore-
headedly,   HORACE GREELEY.
C. A. DANA, Esq., New York.

III.

WASHINGTON, Jan. 8. 1856.
FRIEND DANA: We calculate to elect
Banks in the course of to-morrow night.

No postponement on account of the weather.

I want you to caution your folks not to "hit out" at everything and everybody here, but consider our position. We must have friends, not only in one party but in all parties, or we can learn nothing. My first despatch to you last night about the Democratic caucus was all wrong, because I based it on what Phelps of Missouri told others in my presence, and he did not try to tell the truth. Afterward Barclay of Pennsylvania told me what I telegraphed last, and that is quite a different story— I presume the true one. Now, don't you see that I can't get into Democratic caucuses? I must learn what they do from somebody, and if we pick a quarrel with all opponents personally, what chance have we for news? You remember the Grand Vizier who knocked in the head the Sultan's proposal to exterminate the Infidel dogs, with this sensible demur, "If we kill all the Rajahs, what shall we do for the capitation tax?"

Well, now, I object to Hildreth's personal and savage abuse of old Clayton about his vote on Nebraska in discussing the Clayton-Bulwer treaty. I do not particularly want to use Clayton, but Harvey does, and he is about the best man to pump in the Senate. Seward will rarely tell anything; and, besides, he lives two miles from anywhere. Abusing Clayton so savagely is shying a stone at our own crockery. I would do it if it were provoked; but this was unprovoked. It is a train that don't stop in front of the *Tribune* office, according to Mac's sensible suggestion.

Once more: As we don't want war with England, I would not say that the South won't let Pierce go to war with her—can't be kicked into a war, etc. It will be used by Toombs and other mischief-breeders to push the country as near to war as possible, and they may drive us nearer than they really mean to, and so find themselves unable to back out. Please think of these things, and don't let your people in New York attack persons with whom we are in daily intercourse here, unless there shall seem to be an imperative necessity for it.

Yours,

C. A. D.   H. G.

P. S.—*Tribune* of Monday (just in) says bank suspension took place in '36. It was '37 (May 10). Please correct in Weekly.

I think it wrong to say Catholics, like slaveholders, are opposed to reading the Bible when editions are published by them and urgently recommended by their bishops. I dread all meddling with theology,

IV.

WASHINGTON, D. C., Jan. 10, '56.

FRIEND DANA: We have to-day our first mail from New York for some days. By it I have yours of Monday and Tuesday.

Of course, I know how such things occur as did last Saturday, and I didn't blame you, but I do think Fry is, on the whole, a detriment. He is always doing things too late, and has to be hurried and prompted more than we can afford. And then the annoying folly of filling up the inside of the paper after midnight with that opera rubbish crowding out matter already ancient— I tell you he won't do.

I have labored many years to give the *Tribune* a reputation for candor and generosity toward unpopular creeds and races; and Stewart will use this up if you will let him. It isn't one article on the Jews: he is always slurring them, and this is not like the *Tribune.* I consider even Stewart's anti-Irish articles, though partly true, impelled by a bad spirit, and calculated to make us needless enemies. Let us try to cultivate a generous spirit in all things. Hildreth is a good writer, but he is essentially a Timothy Pickering Federalist of fifty or sixty years ago, and is always fighting the battles of that class of well-meaning but shockingly maladroit politicians. He hates slavery mainly because the South turned out old John Adams. You must gradually teach him to let the dead bury, etc.

We'll elect Banks yet, now you see if we

don't. We made a good push toward it last night. Yours,

H. G.

Let me thank you for your handling of Valk. The man is an ass, but a very malignant one. I trust this letter is genuine.

v.

WASHINGTON, Jan. 17, '56.

FRIEND DANA: I have yours of yesterday. I shall see these treacherous scoundrels through the Speakership, if I am allowed to live long enough, at all events. Our plans are defeated and our hopes frustrated from day to day by perpetual treacheries on our own side. But for these we should have been successful weeks ago. I don't know when we shall come to a result; but there are hopes even for to-day, and better for to-morrow, if no new mine is sprung under our feet, like that exploded by Thorington yesterday. However, that is likely to result, through the caucus, in unintended good.

Since my letters get in somehow, I am less uneasy here, but every traitor and self-seeker hates me with a demoniac hatred which is perpetually bursting out. Lastly your friend, Judge Shankland, General of the Kansas Volunteers, has notified me that he shall cowhide me (for rudeness in refusing to be further bored by him) the first time he catches me in public. Now, I am a hater of novelty, and never had any taste for being cowhided, cowhid, or cowhidden, or whatever the past participle of the active verb used by Gen. Shankland may be, but he is short of funds, and I could not think of putting him to the trouble of chasing me all over the country, so I shall stay here for the present. I trust the man of whom he buys the cowhide will know him well enough not to sell it on tick. I prefer to be the only sufferer by the application.

Yours,

HORACE GREELEY.

C. A. DANA, Esq.

VI.

WASHINGTON, Jan. 21, '56.

DEAR DANA: I send you by this mail a letter from Dubuque which I asked the banker Jesup to write, and which seems to me of greater public interest than most of these local letters are apt to command. As I solicited it, and have kept it several days waiting time to correct it, I hope you will print it soon.

I send also a letter by Ewbank on Dr. Hare's revelations, which seems to me good enough to print. I *did not* solicit this, and am under no obligation to print it. But it seems to me good, though I don't judge between it and the other side. You could easily make it a communication, if you do not want it the other way.

And I mean also to send you by this mail Schuyler Colfax's speech of Saturday, showing up the Democratic argument for a Plurality rule in 1849. This is one of the great hits of the session, and I want you to print it *at once*. It ought to go in the weekly, for it justifies us clear through.

I will try not to bore you with such a load very soon again.

N.B.—" Gen." Shankland's cowhiding not yet come to hand—or back.

Yours,

H. G.

C. A. Dana.

VII.

Washington, Friday Night, Jan. 25.

Dana: I shall have to quit here or die, unless you stop attacking people here without consulting me. You have a paragraph (utterly untrue) from a Boston paper stating that Pennington was in Boston closeted with Gov. Gardner, which was interpreted here as an attack on P. Then comes one from an Ohio paper, classing *Ball* with Moore and Scott Harrison as opposing Banks long after Ball had come back to Banks. And now comes an awful attack on old Brenton, who has been voting steadily for Banks and the Plurality rule for at least two weeks past—certainly since the second nominating caucus. This article will be handed around and read by every shaky man on our side before to-morrow noon, as an evidence of my malignity against every one who ever opposed Banks, and an earnest of what they will all get as soon as Banks is elected. It will hurt us all dreadfully. Do send some one here and kill me if you cannot stop this, for I can bear it no longer. My life is a torture to me.

H. G.

VIII.

Washington, Monday Morning, Jan. 28, '56.

Dana : If you were to live fifty years and do nothing but good all the time you could hardly atone for the mischief you have done by that article on Brenton.

The stupid old dunce had killed himself, and I had decently buried him. After doing all the harm he could, he had come back to us and was voting steadily though sulkily. His power for mischief was at an end, and he could never again have been in a condition to do any. Your savage, blundering attack upon his putrefying carcass has raised it out of the grave and reanimated it with power for mischief. A great testimonial of sympathy and confidence is being got up, and good men are signing it. He is to shine forth a glorified saint tried in the purifying fires of the *Tribune's* malice and falsehood—nay, of *mine*. I have the whole right side of the House upon me— one down, another come on—and I have had to explain the matter separately to each. I had to go to the old animal himself, apologize humbly, and tell him I had telegraphed a contradiction, which would be in Saturday's paper. But Saturday's paper came and no contradiction. I have it in yesterday's Third Edition, but there is probably not another copy of that in Washington, and I have to stand before the House for another day as a liar as well as a libeller. This will go all over the country as an evidence of my bullying falsehood and malignity against any one who ever dared to think of another candidate than Banks.

It will injure the *Tribune* horribly, and enable the old mule to throw away his district in the fall.

Now I write once more to entreat that I may be allowed to conduct the *Tribune* with reference to the mile wide that stretches either way from Pennsylvania Avenue. It is but a small space, and you have all the world beside. I cannot stay here unless this request is complied with. I would rather cease to live at all. If you are not willing to leave me entire control with reference to this city, both men and measures, I ask you to call the Proprietors together and have me discharged. I have to go to this and that false creature and coax him to behave as little like the devil as possible (Lew Campbell, for instance), yet in constant terror of seeing him guillotined in the next *Tribune* that arrives—and I can't make him believe that I did not instigate it. So with everything here. If you want to throw stones at anybody's crockery, aim at my head first, and in mercy be sure to aim well.

We had no mail from New York this morning.

Who takes the responsibility of omitting my despatches when you are away?

We hope to elect Banks to-day.

Yours,

HORACE GREELEY.

C. A. DANA, Esq.

IX.

WASHINGTON CITY, D. C., Jan. 28, 1856.

DANA : You are wrong every way about old Brenton. If you will look through my despatches, you will find that I distinctly stated that he had come back to Banks after the caucus following his bolt, and was voting steadily for him. (I think you will find this not far from a week ago.) You cannot have looked at a number of *The Globe* without finding his name recorded among the voters for Banks, and you ought not to have pitched into him without being *sure* you were right. How did you suppose our vote had gone up so high of late? Besides, you let Ball be attacked in a communication from his district for bolting after he had come back.

You should not have omitted my despatch. Brenton will tell in the House how I promised him and did not perform. It was up in the House to-day, and he promised to bring it up again. He has got Giddings and lots of such to certify for him, and denounce the *Tribune*.

It is very easy for you to make light of this matter in New York, but for me, in the face of thirty double-dyed traitors, ten of them voting against us, and the other twenty cursing me because they can't do likewise, and assailing me every day or two on the floor, it is a different matter. You have terribly weakened our power to hold these villains in check or punish their misdeeds. I wish you had made an editorial correction.

Sadly,

H. G.

X.

WASHINGTON, Wednesday, Jan. 30, '56.

DANA: I retain your note of Scott Harrison. I have no doubt of its truth, and it was well to print it at home, but I think it would do no good to put it in the *Tribune*. He has laid himself open by voting for Dunn's cheating resolves, and there will be abundant opportunities to show him up before spring.

As to —— ——, let his name be mentioned as seldom as possible, and then with suppressed loathing. The little wretch is more malignant and indefatigable than anybody in the House. The night we sat up all night, he acted as whipper-in, waking up Dunn and hunting up Richardson on purpose to prevent a choice. I will enclose ——'s letter to him; but never let him be treated with so much respect as is implied in printing ——'s letter. It will do not the least good, but would elevate the wretch in his own conceit.

The Brenton business has put me under

foot here, and I shall require time to recover. Rust's attack on me yesterday was emboldened, I think, by that. When a man's friends are set against him, he stands a hard chance with his enemies. There are other assaults to follow this. Drunken Bowie of Maryland was threatening me in the bar-rooms last night, and several others; but we are making up a fighting party of Northern men that will ultimately do good. Several pistols will be bought to-day.

Your remarks of yesterday on Brenton are very well, and, now that you are in that fight, you may as well go through with it; but I think I would say little more about it. The article on Lew Campbell was in excellent taste, though I hear he complains of it. Since he required it, it could not well have been better. But an attack upon him would have been a very different thing. I wish you would attack no man or project here without consulting me. Print the facts, and let the comments wait till you can telegraph me. I enclose you a piece of an article from an Indiana paper, showing

what five hundred disclaimers will never stop
—that I am responsible for whatever may
appear in the *Tribune* affecting the House.
The article referred to in this extract was
one of the most foolish and impolitic,
because obviously false, that ever appeared
in the *Tribune.* It tends to exasperate
our enemies, not encourage our friends.

If you had printed my despatches respecting Brenton in all the papers it would have
helped me. I always endorse "private" all
that is not for publication.

Yours,

HORACE GREELEY.

XI.

WASHINGTON, Feb. 1, 1856.

DANA: For God's sake speak the truth
to me. The *Tribune* is cursed all over the
House as having beaten us to-day by your
most untimely article on Bayard Clarke in
yesterday's *Tribune.*

We lost to-day by two votes, and Lew
Campbell wanted to give us the casting

vote, but one would not do it. 'Now, Bayard Clarke had promised to vote for us if his vote would carry it, and in this case it *would* have done it with Lew Campbell's. But when he was called on he would not do it, and gave as his reason your article of yesterday. Of course I am not supposing the false knave would have done it at all; but you have given him what served him as an excuse for not doing it, and the *Tribune* has to bear the credit of beating Banks—for to-day certainly, perhaps forever—in spite of your promise never more to attack any one here without consulting me.

I must give it up and go home. All the Border Ruffians from here to the lowest pit could not start me away, but you can do it and I must give up. You are getting everybody to curse me. I am too sick to be out of bed, too crazy to sleep, and am surrounded by horrors. I shall go to Pittsburgh on the 22d, and I guess I shall not return. I can just bear the responsibilities that belong to me; but you heap a load on me that will kill me.

That article on War and Insurrection in the South is bad in spirit, and does no good. Such will cause the *Tribune* to be stopped in the South.

Yours,

HORACE GREELEY.

XII.

WASHINGTON, Feb. 3, '56.

FRIEND DANA: Of course you understand that the election of Banks was "fixed" before the House met yesterday morning. He would have had three votes more if necessary, perhaps five. There has been a great deal of science displayed in the premises, and all manner of negotiations. A *genuine* history of this election would beat any novel in interest.

I see you are into Dr. Valk again, which perhaps was necessary; but please don't attack any other member of Congress. We got Bayard Clarke's vote yesterday for the Plurality rule, and he didn't vote against us on Speaker, though he had voted for Aiken the night before. We shall want him fifty times this session, and if we only get him ten times it were better so than not at all. Pray allow me to judge with regard to what is passing under my own eyes and not under yours. We are determined henceforth to reclaim Dunn, if possible, and do not despair of the other Filibusters, though Moore voted for Extra Billy Smith, and Scott Harrison promised to vote for Aiken, but backed out. But we shall want all these on Reeder and Kansas.

I would not publish articles about Rust's assault on me, but especially those that speak of my weakness, inoffensiveness, etc. I do not desire any sympathy. At all events I don't wish to beg for it.

Yours,

H. G.

XIII.

WASHINGTON, Feb. 6, 1856.

FRIEND DANA: I had to meet Clayton last evening at Seward's, where I had a quiet talk with him, Col. Benton, and Gov.

S. as to Kansas and what is to be done.
Judge whether it is either pleasant for me
or profitable to the *Tribune* or the cause
to have had him assailed in the *Tribune*
as he was.

I rode home with Col. Benton, who is
every inch as vulnerable as Clayton. But
he is now on the right side, and is doing
good service; would it be wise to attack
him for any of his by-gone errors? And,
above all, should you attack him in New
York in utter disregard of the fact that I
am in friendly understanding with him here?
I want an answer to this, dictated by your
own good sense. How can I exert any influence here, or maintain any position, if at
the very moment I am trying to placate
and win some one you are shying a stone
at him?

I went over this ground before when you
came out so savagely and so mistakenly on
Brenton. You thereupon wrote me that
you would assail no member of Congress
without first consulting me, and yet not a
week elapsed before you come down in full

force on Bayard Clarke, one of the weakest and most excitable men in the House—merely because he had franked a Democratic speech to a constituent. Yet at that very time we were bringing every influence to bear on that same Clarke to induce him to vote first *for* the Plurality rule, and then *not* vote for a Democratic Speaker. He had promised to do what was required. But just then your article came in, and he broke away from all he had promised—voted *against* the Plurality and *for* Aiken. Your attack was his pretext. And had the final vote been taken just then, he would have gone against us, and perhaps carried Valk and Whitney along. And *I* should have been cursed as having defeated Banks, as I had promised that there would be no more of this maladroit warfare. Ought this to have been? Was it consistent with the assurance you had given me?

—Now as to the other matter: I have said nothing about *subscribers* stopping at the South, but the article on British invasion, pointing out the ways and means of

overrunning the South, rousing and arming
the slaves, is calculated to induce the stop-
page of our *mails*—a far more serious matter. Subscribers may please themselves, but
we cannot afford to have an edition taken
from the mails and burnt on a *true* charge
of plotting treason and inciting insurrection.
That article was calculated to excite intense
aversion to us at the South, and is good
nowhere. It implied that we foment Abolition as a means of weakening and destroy-
ing the South—not of regenerating and
upbuilding it. Of course we can have no
friends in the South if we seem to invoke
upon that region the scourges of fire and
sword. And again, by seeking to prove
the South at the mercy of Great Britain, we
virtually challenge all the Hotspurs of that
region to vie with our b'hoys in provoking
a war. You do not want war with England,
and I abhor the thought of it; yet that
article was strongly calculated to foment
one. Do let us make the Southrons see
that we desire Abolition, not because they
opposed the two Adamses, particularly old

John—not for their injury, but for their good.

Of course I don't believe one word in the insurrection programme. Invasion always arouses intense hostility, especially among the lowest strata of society. I believe two negroes would volunteer to fight against an invading force to every one who would flee to their camp. But this is immaterial.

———

I do wish you would consider my position. In yesterday's paper I see you talk of Rust as drunk when he assaulted me. Now, I don't know this and have never asserted it. Of course the barbarian will regard this as a fresh attack upon and defiance of him *by me*, and I can do nothing to undeceive him. I wish you had said nothing of the sort. I doubt that it is just ; I am sure it will tend to harm. Let others denounce or revile Rust : I mean never to speak of him unless obliged to. He is very likely to have trouble here before the session closes, and I must not even be suspected of it.

Somebody in Monday's paper is quite
wrong in saying "the only Know-Nothing,
avowedly such, who voted for Mr. Banks,
was Mr. Edie of Pennsylvania." Edie is a
very poor shote, and President of the Pennsylvania State Council, not the Twelfth-sec-
tion gang, but the other. Every Banks man
from that State but Grow is a Know-Nothing. Robison, J. H. Campbell, Pearce, and
others have avowed it on the floor. Lew
Campbell is eternally boasting of his
"American principles." The Connecticut,
New Hampshire, Rhode Island, and Massachusetts members were all chosen on "American" nominations. It is our policy to sink
the distinction as much as possible, but the
remark above quoted tends to revive and
aggravate it. Please avoid this as much as
possible.

Percy Walker of Alabama is not Anti-
Neb, but *is* Know-Nothing ; Oliver and
Caruthers of Missouri, Talbott of Kentucky,
Watkins of Tennessee, and Bowie of Mary-
land are *not* Know-Nothings, but Anti-K.-N.
Whigs. Cox of Kentucky is not Anti-Neb,

but *is* Know-Nothing; so is Evans of Texas. I cannot guess how these blunders were made, with the *Whig Almanac* at hand. Ohio gives but 17 votes for Banks—you have it 18.

I shall go to Pittsburgh.

Yours,   H. G.

C. A. D.—I can't see how my letter of Sunday should fail for Tuesday's paper, when you have the *Union's* article of same date.

XIV.

WASHINGTON, Feb. 9, '56.

FRIEND DANA: Although this is to me the most detestable spot on earth, I want to stay here through the Reeder fight, if you will let me. I will stand my chances to be horsewhipped or pistolled, if you will keep me clear of being knocked down by the *Tribune.* But bear gently on the K.-N.'s while I have to operate with them here; and pray be careful of letting in such another remark as that none who voted for Banks claim to be K.-N.'s, except Edie.

Such remarks destroy all our reputation for accuracy or sagacity, since it is generally known that the majority of the Banks men are now members of Know-Nothing councils, and some twenty or thirty of them actually believe in the swindle. Half the Massachusetts delegation, two thirds that of Ohio, and nearly all that of Pennsylvania are Know-Nothing this day. We shall get them gradually detached if you will let us; but some of your letters on Gardner, etc., tend to keep them where they ought not to be. Do be circumspect, and draw no lines of discrimination to our own detriment. I am not asking you to *do* anything, only to *forbear* doing what can only work harm. If you have nobody who knows how to classify members of Congress better than the Scandinavian bard, please leave them unclassified. But, in fact, my despatch of last Sunday night stating who were present and did not vote, who threw away their votes, etc., was suppressed, and in its stead Ottarson's budget of blunders inserted as *Tribune* statistics. Now, I don't pretend to

know much; but if I don't better understand what is passing under my own eyes
than any one can who is 250 miles away,
I ought to be recalled and dismissed. But
I have been treated like this throughout.
The *Tribune Almanac* affords no countenance for the blunder of calling Percy
Walker Anti-Nebraska, Bowie and Watkins
K.-N., etc., etc. I cannot see how such
blunders were made. But remember that
I don't expect you to do everything or to
oversee everything. All I ask is that when
*a thing cannot be done right, do not have
it done at all.*

House's telegraph is very near me, and
when you are in doubt as to a Washington
matter, please consult me. Just that in
Brenton's and in Bayard Clarke's case would
have saved me great mortification and injury. You think it isn't hard to say of a
weak man like Clarke that, "not knowing
enough to make a speech, he distributes the
speeches of others." But *he* feels very sore
of it. Besides, it is not a just remark, since
the House is not organized and has yet

afforded no chance to make a speech. Let
the past go, but spare me henceforth.

Yrs.,

H. G.

XV.

WASH'N Sat., Feb. 16.

MY FRIEND DANA: Please *don't* say
such things as the above without consulting
me. They prejudice us, and cannot do any
good. I know this House as you cannot;
and I tell you we have not eighty men
who would vote as this article suggests.
We cannot (I fear) admit Reeder; we cannot admit Kansas as a State: we can only
make issues on which to go to the people
at the Presidential election. Now, the issue
of admitting Kansas as a free State is a
great deal better than that of stopping the
supplies, or anything of the sort. Please
do nothing likely to distract attention from
the main question. And don't lead off on
such an important tack without consulting
me. You see what a handle *The Union*
makes of this to prejudice me.

I wrote last night a letter on Kansas which you will have to suppress or modify, or incorporate with one I shall write to send herewith on future elections in Kansas. *The Union* to-day says our Kansas news are spurious, on which point I am about to write. The differences are not essential, yet they are superficially serious. Chubb, who made up the Kansas article in the Almanac, ought to be blown up. I shall write him about it.

If you see —— in New York soon, make him give you a private account of the Banks election—inside view. —— may be as great a rascal as he is represented : if so, I begin to see the utility of rascals in the general economy of things. Banks would never have been elected without him. He can tell you a story as interesting as the Arabian Nights, and a great deal truer. He has done more and incurred more odium to elect Banks than would have been involved in beating ten Speakers.

I shall try to find some one to write and telegraph while I am gone to Pittsburgh next week—probably Schuyler Colfax. Harvey is good for nothing at our end of the Avenue; his use is at the other.

Yours,

C. A. D.   H.

P. S.—You understand that the letter on Brenton's new certificates, of which I have a proof this morning, is *not* to be published. I only pointed at them and they came down. ,

XVI.

Washington, Feb. 17, 1856.

Friend Dana: I enclose the Banks manifesto in reply to the furious assaults of *The Union* on his committees. I believe it is not in B.'s handwriting, but you will easily recognize the voice of Nathaniel. Please print it on Tuesday (if you can) as editorial, though it repeats some things I have already written. It contains, besides. important facts not before set forth by any one, relative to the packing of committees, and, on the whole, will be good.

You will soon begin to receive letters on Washington society from Bell Smith, who only arrived night before last, and is unwell. If able, she will write two this week —one of them describing the next Levée. It is absolutely necessary to the freedom and piquancy of these letters that *we* should give no hint as to their authorship.

Please correct for me two bad errors in my last letter on Public Lands, on which I have bestowed much labor and thought, and which is to subserve an important purpose.

XVII.

WASHINGTON, Sunday, March 2.

FELLOW CITIZEN : If you received on Friday night my letter on Hale's and Toombs's Kansas speeches, yet allowed it to be crowded out by the immortal scandal of the Griswold Divorce case, why then you failed to consider fairly what is and what is not perishable. My letter would have been middling on Saturday, while it

will be sour as whey and flat as cold dish-
water on Monday; while the Griswold business would have been rolled as a sweet
morsel under the tongues of all the old
maids of New York any day you might see
fit to print it.   But, even if not, your new
allies, the feminine *literati* of our borough
would have sworn the legs off an iron pot
for you in defamation of Rufe any day you
might ask 'em.   And I guess they could
draw from their storehouse other scandals
against that reverend divine quite as racy
as these.   Isn't that so?   I don't object to
a reasonable share of wickedness, but they
had no right to pitch Alice Carey's name
into this business.   It would have answered
just as well to say that Gris threatened to
marry either Miss M. or another lady whom
he named.   Since your old friend, Mrs. E.,
could swear that she did not know her
own age (oh!), she and they might have
been equally chary of Alice's name.

You must not get cross with me.   You
see it seems hard to stay in this dreary,
infernal hole to write letters, which mere

delay makes a great deal more stupid even than they naturally are.

Bell Smith begins to think that you do not want her letters; but I explained to her about the thirty columns. She can write a better series of letters from this town than anybody left here. Have you any suggestions for her?

You keep letting people attack George Law, in spite of my earnest remonstrance. It is a dreadful case of flinging stones at one's own crockery, which you must desist from. George has ceased to be an aspirant and become a patriot. He will never, never give the Hindoo another red cent—nary one. On the contrary, he will help us, if that seems the best means of hitting Fillmore. Why won't you see that such letters as that you printed from Albany about the *Register* play directly into the hands of our deadly enemies? There never was a clearer case of a railroad that did not stop fornenst the *Tribune* office. Oh, my friend the wisdom which teaches what should *not* be said, that is the hardest to acquire of all! I confess my own deficiencies therein, but you must gain more of it.

H. G.

P. S.—Have we got to surrender a page of next weekly to Raymond's bore of an Address? The man who could inflict six columns on a long-suffering public, on such an occasion, cannot possibly know enough to write an Address. Alas for Wilson's glorious speech!

XVIII.

WASHINGTON, Saturday evening, March 8, '56.

FRIEND DANA: I have yours of last night. I can't think there is the least use of saying anything about the Woodworth Planing Machine. I don't know the facts in the case, but I can see that the weight of influence is very heavily against it. I can't believe it has the hundredth part of a chance.

I don't know what the Crowley libel suit means.

I think Pike ought to come here when I leave. When will it suit him to come?

Shall we say the middle of April? I am not particular.

I wish you would humor my prejudices a little, and when I send two or more despatches, not make them into one. For instance, my despatch about the Presidency, in Saturday's paper, had no business jumbled in at the foot of "Kansas in Congress," to which it nowise belongs. Won't you think of this hereafter? I could make my despatches shorter by elisions if I thought they would be read carefully and written out in the office. But when I begin a despatch "Hickman reelected," I count on its being written out, "Mr. Hickman of Pa.;" and when I write "Ohio Campbell," I count on its being written out "Mr. Campbell of Ohio"—and am often disappointed.

As to salary I am indifferent, and, as to the *Tribune*, discouraged. The infernal picayune spirit in which it is published has broken my heart. It was dreadfully important to print the Minority Report and bring up our Washington correspondence on Saturday, yet not a line of all this is in—or

could be without a Supplement. I am
ashamed to meet Bell Smith, after having
at your suggestion asked her urgently to
write us a series of letters, which now can't
get published. I know you do your best,
but you have never seconded me as you
ought in defence of the great principle that
*a daily newspaper should publish everything
as fast as it is ready*, though this should
oblige it to issue two supplements a day.
If you can't do this, better give up the
ghost at once. We ought to have published ten supplements within the past year
—and should have been the richer for it.
We ought to get back to our noble size
soon, and print a supplement at least every
Saturday. No Jew ever managed a pawn-
broker's shop in a baser, narrower, more
short-sighted spirit than the *Tribune* is
managed, and I am heartsick. I would
stay here forever and work like a slave if I
could get my letters printed as I send
them, but the *Tribune* is doomed to be a
second-rate paper, and I am tired.

Yours,

H. G.

XIX.

FRIEND DANA! Don't you see that you made a mistake in printing that Albany letter discrediting the *Register*? Why run down George Law's muskets when they are used to fight our battles?

Let Lew Campbell alone as much as possible. He is a strange creature, but we must make the best of him.

Don't let your folks write more savagely on the Kansas question than I do. I am fiery enough.

I wanted to write to you at length about selling shares to Fry, etc. Do you really wish him to have two, and is he prepared to pay for them? I can't abide the assumption in his letter to me that he is one of the scores of innocent victims of poverty and misfortune who have been working for the *Tribune* for nothing. On the contrary, I think he has received every dollar he has ever earned of us. I apprehend he and I will never think alike on this point, and that we shall make no progress toward an understanding generally.

Yours,

HORACE GREELEY.

C. A. DANA.

XX.

WASHINGTON, March 12, '56.

DANA: I don't scold about the printing of "Indiana Cumback," etc. It only bothers me, because if my despatches are not carefully read and written out, I shall have to write them more fully—which costs money.

I think you ought to have the reports of meetings of Commissioners of Emigration, School Commissioners, etc., set in small type, to save room.

We shall be beaten five to ten (I think) in power to send for persons and papers.

H. G.

XXI.

MARCH 13.

DANA: Be *sure* to print Robinson's Message as early and emphatically as anybody when received. It must be near at hand.

Is Phillips gone back to Kansas? We must have some one there. Can't you have an article on Oude?

XXII.

WEDNESDAY, March 14.

I am opposed to anything that may be deemed a personal warfare upon Fillmore. He is not particularly a candidate, at least in the Free States, but such a fight might make him one. Let the dead rest.

I should like to have nobody assailed personally or generally. I think you mistake in giving Lew Campbell a dig now and then. Never waste ammunition on those who have already committed suicide.

We might make Fillmore a candidate and resuscitate Lew Campbell. But it were better to leave them to their long repose.

H. G.

XXIII.

WASHINGTON, Thursday, March 20, '56.

DANA: Thank you for your note of yesterday. I now see how my letters have been maltreated, and can try to guard against future mischief. That of Friday night was not finished till a little after midnight, and I went down to the office and obtained a promise that it should be taken by the porter to the cars at 6 A.M. Of course that promise was violated, and I have learned that for several nights, *owing to the sickness of a porter!!!* the letters were not taken to the P. O. at night at all, and, of course, mine, which were deposited in the bag in perfect good faith, lay over, while those I took or sent to the cars at 4.30 P.M. went on. You do not speak of mine making an addition to my letter on Clingman, but I know that it was taken to the P. O. in season. I trust you received it so as to amend in the Semi-Weekly.

If any letter fails to arrive by the mail which ought to bring it—as you can easily determine by noticing the date of the papers by the same mail—I wish you would notify me at once. I am really working hard here, and I want the credit of it.

I don't believe in Preston King for President. His Texas votes are in the way. A candidate must have a slim record in these times. I think Fremont or Banks must be put. up—perhaps both.

I look suspiciously at that magazine project, because I regard the *Tribune* as a great idea just begun to be developed, and don't wish anything else to interfere with it. Better do one thing well than several things middling well. To make the *Tribune* the first paper in America is fortune and fame enough for us, and that *we are not now doing*. Let us try to do what we have undertaken before we apply our energies to making picture-books.

I don't understand what you say about T. B.'s letters. I have understood that many more had been sent. I will inquire.

McCormick was here last night and this morning to complain of some grievance at your hands, but I was too busy and had too much company to listen to him then. There is a fierce excitement about Dunn's being or not being on the Kansas Com-

mission.   Banks has just been here, and I
guess he won't go on.

Yours,

HORACE GREELEY.

What are you doing about " Little Dor-
rit"? Don't you mean to print it in the
daily? Seems to me that would be downright swindling of those who have begun to
read it.

XXIV.

DANA: Let me thank you for your glorious issue of yesterday, including Supplement, which I have not yet found time to
read in full, but mean to this evening. I am
obliged for these letters from the growing
towns in the West, every one of which is
worth to us far more than the space it
costs, because it makes friends to our paper
—communities interested in its success. Pray
talk this over with McElrath, and make him
see that I shall not be satisfied till the
editor in charge has authority to issue a

Supplement whenever he has matter in type that he cannot otherwise dispose of. We can get along no other way, and you must help insist on this.

A supplement will not cost more than $300, and, if it were all devoted to such letters as those from Rock Island, Dunleith, etc., it would be worth to us at least $1000. Who can fail to see this?

I am glad, too, that you have printed McCormick's statement, because it seems to be simple justice to him. He has no right to complain (on the whole) of the *Tribune.* But these Mowry people are humbugs, who have done nothing entitling them to one line in the *Tribune.* Their machine may be good—I know nothing about that—but the reputation they won in Europe is naught. Mac is a miser and a bore, and has about as much chance to get his patent extended as to be struck by lightning; but I am glad you have done him justice. I hope it will satisfy him.

Now, have a Supplement every Saturday till the busy season is over. You can

no otherwise do justice to your adver-
tisers.

G.

I will write to Fry to-day, and hope he
will confer with you.

XXV.

WASHINGTON, D. C., March 21, '56.

FRIEND DANA: Thank you for your note
to Bell Smith. She is sick abed for some
days past, and may not be able to write
very soon. But this letter makes all right
between us. I think some of her letters
must have missed, but I am not sure of it.
I called with your letter this morning, but
she was too sick to see anybody.

We *must* have this Supplement matter
settled definitely and soon, in favor of the
right of the editor in charge to put on a
Supplement whenever he has matter which,
in his judgment, cannot be otherwise dis-
posed of. Mac is an excellent business man
in a certain style, but, if he had his way,
the *Tribune* would have been just half-way

between the *Commercial* and the *Mirror* in
circulation, character, and profits. We really
cannot afford to be ruled by this spirit.

So you are beaten on Robinson's message.
I have been fearing that for some time, but
I could devise no remedy. You should
have sent another man so soon as Phillips
came away, or, better, perhaps, have written
to the *Herald of Freedom* to engage one for
us. Don't let this rest another hour. What
did you say to Redpath? I guess he might
have been engaged, if that was desirable.
Remember that the Commission is soon to
go out, and that we must have a good man
attending its sittings, who knows how to
give the material points of the evidence in
full and to condense or suppress the rest.

To be beaten in the morning I suppose
was destiny; but how could you fail to
have it in the Evening Edition? That will
sadly lower our prestige here and elsewhere.

No, my friend, I am opposed to the
Tribune Picture-book. Let us succeed in
what we have undertaken before we try
anything more.

I mean to let you off pretty easily for a day or two, and see if you cannot bring up some leeway. We *must* not suppress our Reviews. If we do, we shall lose our publishers' advertisements, which are about the most interesting feature of our paper. They are almost the only literary luxury I now indulge in.   Yours,

C. A. D.   H. G.

XXVI.

WASHINGTON, D. C., April 2, '56.

FRIEND DANA : I have mislaid your letter to which I replied night before last ; but its tenor might seem to imply a preference on my part for remaining in Washington. I would have it distinctly understood that I am ready to leave this delightful spot the moment you judge that course to be best. I mean to stay as long as that shall be deemed desirable by you ; but I have been expecting some intimation as to a change for some time. Just now Harvey is away and cannot be back till Saturday. When here, he is very good for the Court end of town, but not as to the other. Yet we must have some one here who can write about the Capitol, and I am expecting by each mail to be advised by you of a consignment of Pike. I want him to come prepared to *stay*, as I have done ; merely remaining about here for a week or two is no good. I want him here several days before I leave, so that I can introduce him to some folks who can be of use to him in getting news (his weak point), and to impart to him all I know as to the lay of the land. He can't come too soon to please me, though I am in no hurry. I came here because I could do most good (as I supposed), and don't want to stay one minute longer than that shall be the case. And, though others may be cleverer, there is no correspondent here who has done nearly as much work as I have this winter, except Simonton, and he has great advantages— first, in being always here ; next, in being able to retreat to his den, where he is protected by a barricade of women and children, while my room is the common resort of cigar-smoking, gossiping, political loafers. I began my letter about Washington's tomb after dinner yesterday, and it was close to midnight when I finished it, and had to take it to the post-office, the hotel bag being gone. I could have written it in an hour and a half, but first came in Pomeroy, then Gen. Lane, then Wilson, then Gov. Robinson, besides others, and it won't do to turn such men out of the house. So my time was taken up. And so it is from day to day.

Now about ferocity. I am in favor of it, judiciously applied. Perhaps Douglas is a good subject, but every one is not. If it were practicable to " have a giant's strength," we must be careful not too often " to use it like a giant." A blundering attack like that on Brenton destroys the force of our broadside when better directed. When you show up an Albany *Register* you must consider whether you may not want to use that same—for a lawyer who should make a very strong speech discrediting one of his own chief witnesses would not be

thought clever. And I charge you above all
things not to allow anything to get in which
seems impelled by hatred of the South, or
a desire to humiliate that section. On
the contrary, ours is the course to renovate
and exalt the South, and must be so com-
mended. Every copy of that misjudged
editorial showing how a British army might
liberate the slaves and overrun the South
has been carefully treasured to make Loco
Foco speeches on in the coming canvass,
and I have been applied to for more by
men who did not imagine I knew what
they were after. We must be "wise as
serpents" this season, and make no enemy
needlessly. It is by such articles as Wes-
ton's "Poor Whites of the South," and
making the Kansas issue as prominent as
possible, that we are to win a decisive triumph. There are very many things I don't
begin to know, but I ought to know something of party controversy.

George Baker writes me that he has urged
you to oppose any Excise law, if we can't
have Prohibition. I hope you have done

nothing of the sort. I have no faith in Excise Laws; but we must not take the responsibility of beating one. Let us rather let one pass (*sub silentio*), so as to demonstrate more clearly its worthlessness.

I am disappointed at receiving no letter from Europe this week. Remember to hurry it along when one comes.

Yours,

HORACE GREELEY.

C. A. DANA, N. York.

XXVII.

WASHINGTON, Monday, April 7, 1856.

C. A. D.: I went up to York, Pa., to lecture on Saturday, and could not get back till six this morning.

Thank you for the promise of Pike soon. I am unwell and tired of this hole. I hope he will come down on Saturday at furthest; then I will start on Tuesday and reach home on Wednesday. Ask him to please come down on Saturday, if not earlier. And, when here, I think he must contrive to stay till the 17th of June. Why not? A greenhorn can be of no use here, and Harvey can do us little good at the Capitol. I guess Pike must stay.

Now, as to your going away this summer: There are only two conditions to it. *Somebody* must do up Washington in your absence, and Fry must promise to stand by me and pull steadily in New York. I mean to be extra good this year, and rather doubtful as to the next. So, if somebody will do us justice here, and Fry will really help me in New York, all will be well. (I trust there is to be no opera in those months.)

I guess you are about right as to Bell Smith, except that she couldn't help being found out. As Colfax said to her in my hearing, "*Who else* could have thought of puffing Pugh?" Don't you see that is a settler? All I regret is that you did not write to her on the receipt of her first that you would pay her so and so. It won't do for me to be hiring correspondents, and I only spoke to her because you agreed to it.

Better have a good understanding at the outset. But you don't write notes on such slender provocation as I do.

I presume Seward's speech has been sent you. If not, it shall be by this mail.

—Now, I want to suggest one thing—the hiring of Ewbank to examine *every* new invention that may be presented, and say something or nothing of it, as it deserves. If he has to leave his own house to do so, let those who require it pay him. Otherwise, let him have stated hours three or 'our times a week on which any inventor may call on him, and let whoever comes to the office be told, " Mr. E. is our editor with respect to Inventions. Go to him at ——— o'clock to-day or to-morrow, and he will look into what you have invented and write about it, if he deems it worth notice in the *Tribune.*" We have never yet had this department on a right footing. Ewbank's return to New York gives us a chance ; now let it be done. I think he would do this for one thousand a year, writing a leader, a paragraph, or a mere line about a new invention, according to its merits; but if he asked two thousand, it would be worth the money. Won't you look into this? It would be a great relief to us and a real improvement to the paper.

Yours,

H. G.

P.S.—Contrary to what you would suppose, Clayton was perfectly sober and Bell atrociously drunk at the time of their row in the Senate last week. Bell was a little worse when he undertook to apologize, if possible, than when he gave the insult.

I made a mistake on Friday. Collamer sat down without concluding, while the Senate went to reading and referring bills. So I went into the House to hear Gen. Granger, after which Collamer resumed and concluded. Collamer's speech is better than Seward's, in my humble judgment.

Yours,

H. G.

XXVIII.

Washington, D. C., April 9, 1856.

C. A. D.: 1. I care nothing for Ewbank. If you have the right sort of man to scrutinize inventions, that is well. 2. I don't want more *space* devoted to this subject. I presume quite enough is now given.

But I *do* want inventions treated just like other occurrences—with more or less emphasis, according to their importance—not treated as if a new motive power and a new currycomb were of equal consequence. There your present system is deficient. If a man should invent a new locomotive that could be readily and profitably used in cornfields and on common roads, I should wish to see it announced in a leader on the very day after it was patented ; whereas by your present method it would probably appear the next month in a supplement, buried up under new raspberries and improved bee-hives. Is that the thing ?

I am totally disqualified to judge of the

value of inventions in general; you take little interest in them. I believe the history of Human Progress is written in them; and I want to see that history early and faithfully reflected in our columns. I want to have less and less to do with politics, and more and more with Productive Industry. I feel that the path of Empire—journalistic and all other—stretches in this direction. Let us be first to act on this knowledge, It will win few subscribers to-day, but it will win character which may ultimately be coined, if that is deemed essential. I do believe that our Daily, with five years' reputation as the first to recognize and honor Inventive Genius, would be a far better property than at present.

It does not follow that we should give long accounts of new inventions. Nine tenths of those patented are worthless; three fourths of the residue are of little general interest. One column per week devoted to Inventions will satisfy me, provided the right man prepares it and has a clear idea of what he has to do—that he writes in the interest of the public and not of the patentees.

———

I telegraphed you yesterday about Fremont's letter, and hope you have it in this morning's *Tribune.* It is a good letter in itself, and will do good to Kansas if not to Fremont. I do hope you will have it out soon, and that F. will withdraw his objection, if he has any. I mean to print it in *next* Weekly anyhow, if not in this.

I wish you could have printed Gen. Granger's speech. It will be greatly discussed hereafter, and has the immense merit of being short.

Yours,

HORACE GREELEY.

C. A. D.

XXIX.

WASHINGTON, April 11.

DANA: My heart does not break easily, but these mail failures are hard to bear. On Tuesday Henry Waldron of Michigan made a glorious speech. He is one of our best men, never spoke before, and probably will not again.

I sat down and wrote a telegraphic despatch about it, then a letter. Wednesday's paper came, and no despatch. I wrote one of inquiry to you and took it down to the office, when, lo! they owned up that *they had mislaid and failed to send the despatch till next morning!* So the milk in that cocoanut was accounted for. "Well," says I, "the next paper will bring along *my letter*, anyhow;" but that paper came last night and *no letter*, but instead of that a despatch from you, sent after, saying that the letter only reached you yesterday. Now, I have myself carried every letter to the post-office this week—usually a little before midnight, and the letters are taken till 5 in the morning. So the fault can hardly be here. I am afraid you fail to make a row with the New York Post-office when this sort of thing occurs.

Last night it was 1 o'clock when I took my letter to the office, and your despatch gave me a dread that it might have been overlooked and delayed here. So I have been to the postmaster this morning, and had the office overhauled, and the letter has certainly gone. The only chance of failure is, says the P. M., that these late letters are made up in a special or extra package, and this may be overlooked and left unopened at night in the New York office. Pray look to this.

Your despatch about the Fremont letter is generally admired. I have not yet taken Banks's opinion of it ; but he has written me a note saying that he was misled by A. B. James, and will keep out of such ruts hereafter. Rather late, but very right.

You can't guess how old Butler gave it to me yesterday for that infernal article telling the British how to invade and conquer the South. No report can do justice to his venom. I will try to keep such articles out of the *Tribune* hereafter.

Old Badger was sitting in the Senate all day yesterday. He must be "tickled to death " at the prospect of Pike's return to this city. I trust you have a supplement to

day. Thank Carey in my name for that
article on Bowen. Also, whoever did the
Joe Bonaparte, though it used up so much
room.

I mean to have a weekly or fortnightly
letter from the Patent Office ere-long.

Can't you publish Gen. Granger's speech?
It is unique, and very short.

Yrs.,

H. G.

XXX.

DANA: Will you please have an earnest
talk with Craig? I went to the Senate yesterday on purpose to hear the additional
Crampton documents. On hearing them I
saw that they needed to be sent over ver-
batim, and sent Harvey every way for
Gobright to tell him to send them to the
Associated Press. Harvey came to me and
telegraphed to you on the subject. I found
Gobright and urged him to do the right
thing. He hesitated, but telegraphed to
Craig. Craig answered that he need only
send the substance. I saw Gobright again

early in the evening, and saw him again at 10 o'clock, and he assured me that he had sent all but a few unessential phrases, &c. I could do no more with him, as he was acting under orders from Craig. Now Harvey tells me that you telegraphed at 11 to have *the whole* sent over. Here is a heavy expense imposed on us by Craig's presuming in New York to know more about documents of which he was ignorant than I did after hearing them. I consulted Gen. Webb, and obtained his concurrence before acting. I want you to ask Craig whether I may not expect to be listened to in another contingency like this. Here are at least $500 thrown away by three papers in telegraphing severally what should have gone to all.

G.

XXXI.

LAWRENCE, KAS., May 20, 1859.

DANA: I have been travelling and speaking through Eastern and Central Kansas since last Sunday, when I wrote you from Atchison. I must write again to-night, if possible, though I am nearly worn out with riding a good part of every day, making a speech each day or evening, and shaking hands with everybody.

Besides, I had to make a set speech at Osawatomie day before yesterday, aimed at all manner of political half-breeds and twaddlers, by whom this Territory is cursed, and who are likely to ruin it yet. That speech I have been obliged to write out without a note of help. I finished it at nine o'clock this morning at Prairie City, *and you will have to print it.* It is not so good in the report as I gave it, for I have been hurried and badgered on all sides till I hardly see how I have made time to write it at all; and some of its best points are entirely omitted for want of notes and time. However, you will think it too long; but I shall probably bore you little more for two months, or till I reach California. Just put this through, then; for there is considerable malignity in it, some of which will seem funny to some folks and not so funny to others. In Kansas, where its every shot will hit somebody, I know it will do good, and I promise not to write out another this side of San Fran. at the worst.

Rain—mud most profound—flooded rivers and streams—glorious soil—worthless politicians—lazy people—such is Kansas in a nutshell. Good-night.

Yours,
HORACE GREELEY.

CH. A. DANA, Esq., New York.

XXXII.

June 14.

I am still lame and suffering, but hope to be able to push on next Monday. I shall try to send by this mail a new letter (the last) on the Rocky Mountain gold region.

I am still lame, having rather a bad gouge in my leg (with the corner of a wagon seat when I was upset), but I mean to get away toward Laramie to-day or to-morrow. I must pay $100 to be carried 180 miles—rather steep. It is horribly hot here, everything parched and drooping, and I am not satisfied with the treatment of my leg. I hope

to find better at Laramie. There is no
house between this and that, and I expect
to be six or seven days reaching Laramie.
We shall be bothered with some of the
larger creeks issuing from the mountains,
which are swelled by the melting snows.

I have seen no later *Tribune* than May
23, nearly a month ago. I hope to find
some at L.

H. G.

XXXIII.

DANA: This letter is a sort of *résumé* of
my last six. If you are crowded, and find
it in good part consists of repetitions, you
may offer it to Bonner or some one else;
and, if they don't want it, keep it for me.
I shall write another on the gold mines.

I am still intent on curing my lame leg.
I shall not be able to reach Laramie much
before the 1st of July, when I intended to
be at Salt Lake on the 4th. But I can do
nothing with my wound while travelling. It
was made by the corner of a seat gouging
into the side of my left leg, just below the
knee. It is now improving.

LETTERS
TO A LADY FRIEND.

PREFACE TO LETTERS TO A LADY FRIEND.

IF we except Abraham Lincoln and Benjamin Franklin, there is hardly another so individual and piquant a personality to be found in American history as that of Horace Greeley. What a strong, effusive character he was—autochthonous, and unique in many ways. The good-nature and beneficence and homely philosophy of the two great men we have classed with him were qualities that he, also, eminently illustrated. We .may differ in opinion with such men as these, as we sometimes must; but we cannot easily doubt their inherent nobleness and sincerity. Their very style of speech revealed their downright, straightforward meaning. Hypocrisy was as foreign as generosity was natural to each of them. In the search for truth it was the real meaning of a thing—or, to use Matthew Arnold's phrase, "to see the thing as it, in itself, is" —that was the end of all their studies and mental quests.

Mr. Greeley may not have kept up the Plutarchan parallel one is tempted to draw, in steady balance of mind, or in certain other qualities, with either his illustrious predecessor or with his famed contemporary with whom I have compared him; but he completes with them a somewhat homogeneous trio, the like of which, I imagine, it will take more than another century of our national existence to repeat for us.

Mr. Greeley's pen was surely not always velvet-footed. He gave heavy blows in a time when the amenities of journalism were not even thought of. Resentments were engendered, often, and it is not the nature of resentment to be judicial. On account of these, perhaps,—though he lived before the public with a frankness equalling the fidelity of his utterance,—he was, occasionally, one of the most egregiously misrepresented persons of his time. There were a few chosen friends, who shared in a close intimacy with him, who could at any time have corrected the uncharitable inferences that gained currency about his alleged ambition, and who knew that the loss of the Presidency did not seriously disappoint or affect him. But —so little has their opinion prevailed—it is still popularly supposed by many that he died on account of his defeat. On the contrary, there has probably never been a man defeated in the struggle for that high place who did take, or could have taken, the disappointment with a more cheerful philosophy.

Two years before the Presidential election of 1872, as I happen to know, his health was badly broken by the results of malarial poison. I doubt if he ever quite recovered from its malign effects. Yet he was, in spite of this serious affliction, persistently overworking, as usual, when he needed absolute change and rest. During the campaign he was never idle. Such letters as he wrote were with his own hand; and he was even writing for a cyclopædia, among other tasks,—to say nothing of enduring the tiresomeness of greeting and shaking hands with thousands of people for the long six months of his candidacy. He was at different times travelling and making speeches. When he was upon that famous Western tour, near the end of the Presidential campaign,—marvellous for his twenty and more speeches a day from the railroad platform, and no one of them repeating another,—it was currently said that he "tired almost to death" the young representatives of the press who followed to report him. This tour was hardly ended, when it became apparent that his wife was slowly dying; and for weeks he lost sleep in his anxiety over her situation. Then a conspiracy to take the *Tribune* from him followed. Is not here enough to account for the destruction of two or three men? But malevolence must have its say, and it has been busy saying that he died from disappointed ambition.

During the campaign spoken of—as well as before it—Mr. Greeley was engaged in a remarkable private correspondence with an esteemed friend, a correspondence which let

everything be spoken. In fact, its freedom
was so great that passages in these letters
can never properly be printed. Fortunately,
they happen to throw some light upon the
matter of his ambition, and illustrate the
man in more than one retrieving direction.
These familiar and friendly letters have been
confided to me to edit, and to publish, so
far as they can be reasonably exhibited to
public scrutiny. They are offered by the
person to whom they were addressed, in the
belief that they will do him credit, and help
.—where he has been maligned—to give the
truth which will prove to be his vindication.
The person to whom they were written is a
lady of remarkable judgment and intelligence; and she was, perhaps, the most intimate friend and acquaintance of all Mr.
Greeley's later life. Of this attachment—
formed first through religious sympathies—
she was eminently worthy. By her benevolent character, her keen discernment, and
her sunny spirit, she drew, and still holds, a
social circle of noted people about herself,
who cannot say too much of her philosophy

and virtues. She shrinks with natural delicacy from having her name connected with this presentation, but gives me—except a command not to omit certain paragraphs which she has named in the correspondence —the widest latitude in its preparation. The task, as I saw from the first, requires a nicety of judgment which I trust I have not overstepped.

The letters are arranged below in chronological order. I have made in them only such omissions as seem absolutely necessary, and which are indicated. Here for the last few years of his life Horace Greeley laid his whole heart open to be read as an open book. They constitute unquestionably the most unreserved correspondence he ever indited. Written in haste, in moments of fatigue,—sometimes in the midst of a rapid journey, and hardly ever with the benefit of leisurely composition,—they furnished for him the most welcome communion and relaxation he ever had. It cannot be possible that the public will not read them with keen interest and rise from their perusal with an enhanced admiration of the man. The recent sad destruction, too, of so many of his papers by the burning of his daughter's house at Chappaqua will make more rare and welcome these utterances, as well as whatever else is left, in any new quarter, to add to his history.

J. B.

LETTERS TO A LADY FRIEND.

I.

New York, September 24, 1870.

My Friend: I found at Gloucester what seems to be my fate,—hard work. Going into the Convention [Universalist] I listened to the report of a committee which had been chosen last year to prepare and submit reformed constitutions for the denomination throughout. There was instantly developed a strong opposition, which seemed intent on talking the Convention into a postponement as nearly indefinite as might be. So I took hold for the committee and made myself a general nuisance by insisting that delegates should speak to the question or subside, by calling incessantly for a vote instead of mere talk, and by moving the previous question whenever I could with any hope of being sustained. The result was that I

167

made some enemies, but the constitutions, slightly amended, were all carried and sent to the State Conventions for approval and ratification.

This took nearly all my time, and I at last ran out of the Convention to snatch my valise and strike for the cars.

Wednesday morning we adjourned to hear Dr. Miner's sermon, and that was *all* the sermon I heard in Gloucester. I heard none of the popular speeches.

Wednesday afternoon from three to five o'clock I devoted to looking for you, standing on high ground between the streams of people from the tent and from the mass meeting outside, where they met to take the way back to Gloucester; but, while I saw almost every one, including Rev. —— looking hard for his wife, I recognized no face [from your town]; and so, at 1.35 on Thursday, I came off, having business at Salem which compelled me to take the owl train from Boston at 9 P.M.

I hope we shall meet again ere many months, but I cannot join the pilgrims to

Good Luck, as I start for St. Louis at 9 P.M. of Tuesday.

I did not see you yesterday—or rather you did not find me—because I was obliged to visit my farm, and that took all day. But I received your friend's note on my return last night, and beg her to receive this with thanks as my response. Tell her it is the only letter among at least thirty received together that I have yet found time to answer.

That health may bless and happiness crown your days, and that these may be long in the land, is the fervent prayer of

Yours,

HORACE GREELEY.

II.

GREELEY, COLORADO,
Thursday, October 13, 1870.

MY FRIEND: I have been a fortnight (almost) wandering through West Virginia, Ohio, Missouri, Kansas, etc., to this place, where on my arrival from Denver to-day I found your welcome letter,—none among

the many awaiting me *more* welcome, except that of my daughter I——, informing
me of her safe arrival in London with her
invalid mother, who seemed scarcely the
worse for the long and ill-advised journey.

Let me give you some idea of this place
and people.

Between the main branches which form
the river Platte, several smaller rivers or
large creeks issue from the eastern base of
the Rocky Mountains, and, after a short
cruise over the Plains, fall into the North
or the South Platte. The largest of these
is the Laramie; next comes the Cache à
Poudre, which rises in the snowy range near
Long's Peak and runs nearly 'due east into
the South Platte, about half-way of its
course over the Plains. The new Denver
Pacific Road connecting the Kansas Pacific
at Denver with the Union Pacific at Chey-
enne crosses the Cache à Poudre five miles
above its junction with the South Platte,
and here is located around the railroad station, which has as yet no dépôt, the new
village of Greeley, youngest cousin of Jo-

nah's gourd. The location was pitched upon by the locating committee of our Union Colony about the 1st of March last, the land secured soon afterward, and the settlers began to arrive on the bare, bleak prairie early in May. There were no buildings, and nothing whereof to erect them, and the soil could not be cultivated to any purpose without irrigation; yet here we have already some seven hundred families, three hundred houses built or nearly finished in the village, one hundred more scattered on the prairie around, and probably two thousand persons in all, with more daily arriving. We have an irrigating canal which takes water from the Cache six miles above and distributes it over one thousand acres, as it will do over several thousands more; and we are making another in the north side of the Cache very much longer, which is to irrigate at least twenty thousand acres. We are soon to have a newspaper (we have already a bank), and we calculate that our colony will give at least five hundred majority for a Republican President in 1872,

after harvesting that year a wheat-crop of
not less than fifty thousand bushels, with
other crops to match. And we hope to in-
cite the foundation of many such colonies
on every side of us.

But enough of this. I spoke to the colo-
nists in the open air yesterday, traversed
the settlement and examined its canal, to
the head, and leave this morning on the
train for home, where I hope to be, thank-
ful for a safe and rapid journey, on Monday
evening next. This letter would reach you
sooner if I carried it, but I wish it to bear
the proper post-mark, and to show you that
I write at sunrise, looking off upon the
Rocky Mountains, which present a bold and
even front some twenty-five miles westward,
with Long's Peak about sixty miles off as
the crow flies, and many others covered
with eternal snow glistening behind and
around it. Excuse great haste, for I have
much to do before leaving at 9.45, and believe me ever

Yours,

HORACE GREELEY.

III.

NEW YORK, February 28, 1871.

MY FRIEND: I have refrained for a week from thanking you for the happy day I had at J——, and which I should probably have missed but for you. Mrs. R——'s eyes were very pathetic, but I am hardening myself to say "No" to such; but the thought that you would be glad to see me in your village on the occasion decided me to go. And my reward was the only day in many months that was one of enjoyment and not work. For this—though I believe I first volunteered to go, as I did to speak —I give all my thanks to you.

Seeing Barnum at church on Sunday, I asked him about your expected visit, and he said he thought you (and Mrs. R——) would come to his house whenever I would. But he had not seen your mother, which I had, and I am so accustomed to sickness that is serious that I apprehend your mother may not be able to spare you while the weather

remains capricious and at times severe as in
our March. I do not know how old your
mother is; but she looks over seventy, and
if so her hold on life cannot be firm. Now,
I want you to be without care and unlikely
to be called suddenly home when you visit
our city, and this involves your mother's
complete restoration and reasonable assurance that her good health will endure.
Please let me hear what is the prospect,
and when we may expect you to come over
resolved to remain not less than two Sun-
days at least. I am anxious, if the weather
should permit, that you should be one of a
small party to visit my country home (where
nobody lives) and see what a nice place it
would be if only good people actually *did*
live there.

But I am forgetting that my pen-marks
are hard to decipher, for which forgive me,
and good-by.

Yours,

HORACE GREELEY.

IV.

NEW YORK, March 17, 1871.

MY FRIEND: I have your letter of the
15th, but will not yet abandon the hope of
your visit. I saw when with you that your
mother was likely to be quite sick; but
spring is a great restorer, and I will hope
to hear that she is well again, and that you
will come to see us. If you can obtain
another copy of the J—— paper, please cut
out the account of your dedication and
inclose it to me. Mr. Barnum received the
copy you sent him, but mine failed. I infer
that the *Tribune* office devoured it. I
would like to see it.

I am very glad that my remarks satisfied
your judgment. At the time it must have
seemed presumptuous and even intrusive in
me to offer to speak when no one asked
me, but I felt that some things needed to
be said that others would not be likely to
say, so I volunteered; and I think what I
said would make the orthodox regard our

little band more kindly. Since you approve, I am doubly glad that I offered to speak.

I do not reconcile myself to Br. R——'s bodily weakness. It seems to me that he has no right to be an invalid. I must speak sharply to him on the subject when we meet again.

I shall surely try to visit J—— again, even though you never come to see us. No doubt I shall find an excuse where the will is so good.

With kind remembrance to all friends, I remain   Yours,

HORACE GREELEY.

V.

NEW YORK, April 2, 1871.

MY FRIEND: Mr. Barnum is sick,—has been so for more than a week,—which explains his not answering your last. I called on him this morning, and found him so much better that he hopes to be out to-morrow.

He unites with me in hoping that you

may be able to come and see us this week,
—Thursday if possible. I will meet you at
the ferry if I may know when to expect
you. Next Sunday is Easter,—a great day
here,—and my daughter is to be out of
school all next week. We are going up to
Chappaqua in force on Saturday if that
should be a good day. I profoundly hope
that you may be able to be one of us. I
will not urge you, but we shall be a happier party if your mother's health and
your other duties shall enable you to join
us. At all events, let me hear from you,
and oblige   Yours,

                        HORACE GREELEY.

VI.

NEW YORK, April 5, 1871.

MY FRIEND: I have yours of the 3d.
I hoped that you could come to spend a
few days with us. Now that this is not to
be, I am convinced that all is for the best.
I should have been too busy to see much of
you, except on Saturday and Sunday, with

half an hour at breakfast on other days;
and I wished to meet you under better
auspices. Yet I can't attend the General
Convention [Universalist] next September
at Philadelphia, where you are sure to be,
since I must then be in the West. Next
month I go to Texas. So, you see, my life
is all a fevered march, and I now seem
unlikely ever to sit down and have a quiet
talk with you. (I have some dry cedar
wood up at Chappaqua, which I have long
purposed to burn in an open fireplace on
a succession of winter evenings, while I sit
before it with a few dear friends, read
poems, and talk over our past lives. But
I guess that cedar will remain unburned
till after my funeral.)

I regret to find you inclined to disparage
yourself. There are but two kinds of people
on this planet,—those who try in some
humble way to do good, and the other
sort. The former are all equals, and
should so regard themselves, as well as each
other. I have no friends who would not
be happy and proud of your acquaintance.

Well, I shall take my daughter G—— (now fourteen, almost) and go up to Tarrytown on Friday evening to see a good friend, and then over to Chappaqua next morning, even though it rain. I hope to have a long, bright day there. And so, dear friend, adieu, and believe me

Yours truly,

HORACE GREELEY.

VII.

NEW YORK, April 20, 1871.

MY FRIEND: I have yours of the 18th, and thank you for so good an excuse for saying that I and my baby (almost fourteen) had a very choice Saturday at Chappaqua. We went up to Tarrytown on Friday evening to visit dear friends, then drove across (ten miles) to Chappaqua. The day was bright and quite warm, as you know. A friend and his daughter accompanied us, and brought us back in the afternoon to Tarrytown, whence we came home that night. I remember few days more entirely enjoyable.

I went up again last Saturday, but the day was dull, and many things went awry. I lost my pocket-book coming down, telegraphed two ways for it, and it was thereupon found in the Sing Sing depot; but I did not receive it till yesterday, and meantime I had two places to speak, for one of which I relied upon my memorandum in diary and had hard work to find the place. I was befriended by a good Providence in that, as in finding my pocket-book after it had lain three hours in a busy depot unnoticed. So, on the whole, *that* visit turned out well. I go to Texas reluctantly. There seems no choice but to be in the world or out of it. I am not sufficiently broken down to refuse to bear my part among men: so I keep on. It will be just the same a hundred years hence.

You judge that men will not suffer forever. If to suffer implies *pain*, I agree with you. In the sense of *loss*, I think suffering will endure. That is, I believe the *very* wicked here will never be quite so well off as though they had been good,—that they

will never make up the leeway they lost
while serving the enemy here. I judge that
Mary Magdalene is now, and ever will be, in
a lower grade than Mary the Mother of
Jesus. As to the Scriptures, please consider
Daniel xii. 3. I do not insist that this re-
fers *specially* to the future life; I only urge
that it indicates the *general* principles on
which the divine government rests. So of
all that speaks of "rendering to every man
according to his works." These passages
may not *specially* apply to the future life;
but their *spirit* pervades all God's dealings
with men.

I *did* send you *The Independent*, wishing
you to see what I hold.

I hope your friend's visit gave you real
pleasure, and that you will yet visit your
friends in this city, and never fail to count
among them

Yours,

HORACE GREELEY.

IX.

NEW YORK, Tuesday, May 9, 1871.

MY FRIEND: I dropped in at Mr. Barnum's this morning to bring away some things I had left there, and inquired if they had heard from you. He gave me your letter, and I learned that I would have one, which has just come with my mail. I hoped you would write, but did not request it, wishing it to be your own unprompted act. I should have written you before starting for Texas at any rate.

I leave on Thursday morning. Two friends go along, out of pure kindness, though I did not request it. One of them means somehow to make the journey pay, but will go anyhow. The other seeks no advantage save the journey. I go by Pittsburg, Cincinnati, New Orleans, and Galveston, and expect to be gone nearly or quite four weeks.

I went to Mamaroneck to lecture the day you left us. If it did not rain that evening, I don't see how it could. We had a thin house, but they all had to stay to the end, as the falling rain was even harder to endure than the lecture. Of course I had nothing to complain of; but it was rather a chilling performance for the rest.

On Saturday I went up to say good-by to Chappaqua. It was cloudy, and everything drowned in rain; but none fell there while I stayed, though it rained heavily here in the afternoon. In the evening I had to make a tariff speech to a rainy-day audience at the Cooper Institute. This was rather a colder affair than the day at Chappaqua, though that was rendered gloomy by contrast with the sunshine and your presence on the previous Saturday. I went up to my own woods, to see where a part of them had been burned over by a careless fire a few days since. On the whole, my last Saturday at Chappaqua was not a success.

When you receive this, I shall probably be moving off to Texas at a good rate. I hope to return in good condition and to meet you again before the year closes. Mr. Barnum will try to have you and Mrs. R—— visit

him at Bridgeport in the summer, and I
have promised to spend part of the time
there if you do.

My friend, I charge you not to disparage
yourself, and especially not to regret that
you do not, when I have the pleasure of
seeing you, talk mainly philosophy or epi-
grams. I have a large acquaintance with
those who are regarded as brilliant women.
They appall and fatigue, while you charm
and cheer me. I pray you not to be like
unto them.

Yours,

HORACE GREELEY.

X.

NEW YORK, July 24, 1871.

MY FRIEND: I thank you for yours of
the 19th inst. at hand. I make it an excuse
for sending you one of Fredericks' profile
photographs, because you approved a larger
one like it which my children keep in their
dining-room at Chappaqua. It is not a good
likeness, but that does not diminish its
comeliness.

G—— reached her mother and sister on the 6th. She had ague on the way and on the day of her arrival, and the [here a few words are absolutely illegible], who were counted on to care for her, paid her no attention whatever. A kind German couple took an interest in her, finding she had gone alone to a hotel at Southampton, and saw her safe at her destination in London, where her feeble, suffering mother was overjoyed at her coming. I have only heard once, by a letter from I——, since G—— arrived, but must hear soon again. They have hired a furnished house in London till September 1st, but nothing is decided as to their movements beyond that. Both children want to come home, but will do whatever their mother's health shall suggest as best for her.

I wrote you soon after I returned from Texas, and cannot guess how the letter failed to reach you. It was not worth intercepting.

I was sick when I ought to have written my Akron address, and it was unfinished; but I know it was sound in doctrine and said what was needed. It has stirred up many adverse criticisms.

Please remember me kindly to Mr. and Mrs. R——, and believe me

Yours,

HORACE GREELEY.

XI.

NEW YORK, August 17, 1871.

MY FRIEND: I am to talk temperance at New Egypt. next Wednesday, and I expect to pass through J—— on the morning of that day. I shall not have time to call, but I should like to shake hands with you at the depot, if that does not give you too much trouble.

I enclose a photograph of my daughter I——, which I can only lend you, as I want it returned. I hope you will know her hereafter. Her life has been given to her invalid mother and has been a hard one; but you will see that trial has not hardened her nature nor soured her disposition. I am flattered when told that she looks like me, though I can hardly see it.

Did I write you about G——'s journey to London? You know she had fever and ague last fall, and again this spring, and it broke out again on the ocean and made her trip a miserable one. She landed alone and [was ill] on her way to London. She wrote me soon afterward that the London doctors knew nothing of treating fever and ague; but Ida writes her [attacks] are at last broken, at which I rejoice.

Hoping I may have a glimpse of you next week, I remain

Yours,

HORACE GREELEY.

XII.

New York, Monday, August 28, 1871.

MY FRIEND: I want you to assure the P——s that I usually behave better than I did last Thursday. I absolutely needed to go away and rest when I found that there was no use for me till after dinner.

Those dripping woods at New Egypt had given me a chill, whereof the net result

was neuralgia in my teeth, and I was not
fit to be about, so I seemed selfish and
rude, when I was really sick and suffering.
Then I had to ride to Bordentown, then
to lecture there in an open wood at night,
from a stand ten feet above the people's
heads,—and of course not one tenth of the
vast crowd could hear a word. After lecturing in this absurd way, we drove up to
Trenton, and by this time I was very sleepy
and my night's rest was lost. Next morning I came home in a pouring rain and set
to work to make up for lost time. It
rained so Saturday morning that I could
not go up to Chappaqua, which gave me
time to bring up my arrears of work; and
to-day I have gone to work in earnest to cure
my neuralgia. Saturday I must go to the
farm, rain or shine, and Sunday evening I
start for the West. And so you see why I
don't read many novels.

I had not received yours enclosing I——'s
photograph when I saw you, though I said
I had, misunderstanding your question. I
have it now, and shall take the picture

with me. Photographs are not those they represent, but are better than nothing.

With kindly regards for your brothers and all friends, I am

                 , Yours,

                     HORACE GREELEY.

XIII.

DUBUQUE, IOWA, Sept. 24, 1871.

MY FRIEND: Do you care to hear further about those poor old teeth? I think I wrote you that I was leaving New York an invalid, with my face bound up in cotton bandages, neuralgia rampant, and generally out of repair. I had to ride all the three next nights, with one of the intervening days, stopping to speak the other day, and did not gain much; but after that I travelled more leisurely, and soon wore out my torment, by the help of dentists and their severe but transitory afflictions. Since then I have been travelling and speaking in comparative comfort, through Wisconsin, Minnesota, and Iowa, which last I leave to-

morrow morning. I speak twice in Illinois
and twice in Northern Ohio, and hope to be
at home one week from to-day.

Except a few scowling, threatening days
in Minnesota, I have enjoyed delightful
weather.   But for riding nights and speaking out-doors at fairs, I should almost enjoy this vagabond life.   But when I ride
all night, and speak in the daytime, as at
Des Moines, devoting the intervals to hand-
shaking, etc., I get so weary sometimes that
I can hardly stand up.   Then I feel the
weight of fifty years as I do not when
fairly treated.

I have letters from I——, saying that it
is decided that they do not come home this
fall, but go to the South of France for the
winter.   Perhaps this is best, as mother is
so weak that I—— dare not trust her to
cross the ocean.   She writes that she is very
homesick, and means to come in the spring
whether or no.   I do hope you will yet
know I——.   There may have been better
among us, but they are gone.   She remains
to attest the possibilities of our kindred.

Of course you have been to the Convention, and seen many friends there, beside those you made. I would have attended if I could.

I heard a lady (Miss Wilkes) preach in the Universalist church at Rochester, Minn., last Sunday, and she did well. I talked temperance that evening, and she assisted. I attended the Universalist church here this morning.   Yours,

HORACE GREELEY.

XIV.

NEW YORK, Oct. 7, 1871.

MY FRIEND: I returned from the West last Sunday morning, having spoken twice each day—once to immense crowds in the open air, and each evening (on politics) at great length in halls—on the 28th and 29th ult.; then started (from Youngstown, Ohio) and rode straight home. My throat was rough as a saw, but I came home in far better health and strength than I left. In fact my work here is harder and more

monotonous than any other, and my last
week's incessant writing has set me back
more than a month of travelling and speaking.

My folks are in Paris, on their way to
Arcachon, near Bordeaux, where they expect to spend the winter in a hotel in a
pine forest, in a very mild, health-giving
climate. It was the best they could think
of, but may not prove all they painted it.
In the spring they will come home, D.V.
I—— and G—— take turns in caring for
their helpless, suffering mother, who is dis-
abled by rheumatism from walking or even
standing, though mind and voice are strong
as ever. I grieve for I——'s worn anxious
youth, which can never be regained, though
she does not think of it.

I have had a bright day at Chappaqua
to-day, after five weeks' absence. Lonely as
it is, it looks like home.

Which reminds me to say that I only
write this because your letter just received
intimates a doubt that allusion to my son
would be agreeable. Two sons, who at-

tained the ages of five and a half and six years respectively, have gone before me, and of whom I cherish none but tender and pleasant remembrances. The older, " Pickie," was a poet, the most beautiful child I ever saw, with the bluest eyes and the most heavenly golden hair I ever saw. I walked through the great Italian galleries two years after he was called away; but none of the great painters had ever *seen* a child so lovely. My later son (Raphael) lived to be six months older than Pickie, and was also beautiful in soul and body, but more like me than like his brother, and not a poet at all,—only a very good, bright, noble boy. I seldom find time to think long of either now, but always recall them with sunny memories and a cheerful trust that they are awaiting me with love and trust.   Yours,

HORACE GREELEY.

XV.

New York, Oct. 24, 1871.

My Friend: I have not many friends. My life has been too hurried, and too much absorbed in pressing duties and anxious cares. Of my few friends most are women ; and these I am proud of. Some of them were school-mates, and know all that may be truly said in my dispraise. I wish to hold you permanently enrolled among them, because hardly one of my older friends are in full religious sympathy with me. Even —— has gone to the Catholics, as has [the only one] with whom I am in intellectual rapport; and so, as I grow old and weary, I need you as the one woman who can understand and appreciate my reveries concerning the Unseen World.

I am right glad that you were here to hear Parepa, though I did not meet you. I am not regularly at the office, though frequently there. Yet, should you ever visit our city again, I wish you would advise me of your coming, so that I might find you if that were possible.

I chanced to meet Barnum, full of his success in money-making, some two weeks ago, as I was going to Chappaqua. (He was going up to Bridgeport.) Probably it was the very day you came here.

I have never seen Parepa (I believe), nor Nilsson, nor even Ristori. I have seen no opera since I went with you. I *did* go to see Miss Cushman last week, because my sister asked it, and because I knew her so many years ago. But, as I went alone, and the other actors were poor, I had rather a lonely evening. I *must* hear Nilsson—but when?

I have no word from my folks since they left Paris on their journey to the southwest of France. They would travel slowly, halting at Tours and at Bordeaux. I should have heard from them at Arcachon ere this, and their silence augurs a slow and difficult journey.

G—— wrote from Paris to a friend that she enjoyed that city, with only the drawback of her mother's sufferings, and had found her "better half" in a young girl, daughter of a family who spent last winter in the Isle of Wight. She will find it very dull at Arcachon, with a poor chance of getting that variety of delicate food required by my suffering wife.

And so good-night, my friend, whom I claim not more for myself than for the daughters who shall survive me.

Yours,

HORACE GREELEY.

XVI.

NEW YORK, Nov. 14, 1871.

MY FRIEND : We have had an election since I received your letter, and I have had bad news from my family, but later advices left them in improved health. But they have made a bad choice of a wintering-place,—Arcachon, near Bordeaux, near the southwest corner of France, which the high winds of the Bay of Biscay sweep fearfully in winter. They threaten to "move on" six hundred miles or so,—perhaps to Nice, and perhaps to Italy itself. The children are worn out with travel and thoroughly home-sick, but everything bends to the hope of retaining their mother in this sphere, and making her life as bearable as may be. I think, however, they will all come home in the spring.

*   *   *   *   *

I wish it were possible for me to find rest this side of the grave, but it seems not to be. Work crowds me from every side. I do not seek it, but it comes. If I could be voted out of the editorship of the *Tribune* I could limit the rest of my work; but this seems to draw after it incessant applications to do more on every side, and there is no escape. Shall we never find time to talk of matters of higher and enduring moment? I have been chopping at Chappaqua every Saturday of late, and I have a lot of red cedar cut up into firewood and well sea-soned. You know how pleasant is the odor of burning cedar. Well, I reserve this to warm and light my hearth when I can—at

some future day, with my family about me
—go up and spend three or four consecu-
tive evenings, long bright evenings, reading
choice poems, and discussing higher themes
than those which engross such dreary letters
as this from

Yours,
HORACE GREELEY.

XVII.

NEW YORK, Nov. 26, 1871.

MY FRIEND: *   *   *   *

We can consider this matter buried forever. I can surrender living friends, if I
must; I must be faithful to the memory of
the dead.

Now give heed to a matter on which I do
not wish any one's good opinion but your
own. . . .

But here am I at the head of a newspaper which is a great property, which
others mainly own. If it were all mine I
might not mind the risk; but it belongs to
others, and I must be seriously damaged by

the course I am inclined to take. Moreover, if I take that course, I shall be widely believed to have thus sacrificed others' property to my own personal resentment,—perhaps to my own ambition.

Such is my perplexity,—such the complex problems which active life is constantly proposing. Take a week to think of this, and write me your conclusions. You like my G——; so do I. . . . The call for her to cross the ocean was urgent, and she was even more prompt than I to respond to it.

So you say that I am advertised to speak in Jersey on Thanksgiving Day? If so, it is a mistake. I start eastward to-morrow morning to lecture four times in New England, and hope to visit "the cot where I was born" on Thanksgiving Day, which I make a full holiday. So please note if that day be fair and mild, in which case I hope to make it one of enjoyment with the children of my father's oldest sister.

Yours,

HORACE GREELEY.

XVIII.

NEW YORK, Dec. 4, 1871.

MY FRIEND: *   *   *

If I do not dare, do not forget my reasons. And yet it is possible that I may dare. . . . I shall stay at home the next coldest day of the year.

Next to my birthplace' I called on an old lady, formerly my mother's next friend, who was present at my birth, and then thirty-two years old. My talk with her made me feel quite young. She is not so gray now as I am, and hardly older in mind or body. But my brother's old orchard is in the last stage of dilapidation,—my mother's favorite tree utterly vanished.

News to-day from my folks. . . . I—— means to get away by herself and take a run down to Italy for two or three weeks. I wish she would revere Rome more and the Pope less, but I hope she will go anyhow.

And so good-night, for it is very late,

and my leader on the message yet to proof-
read.   Yours,

HORACE GREELEY.

XIX.

NEW YORK, Dec. 25, 1871.

MY FRIEND: Your last reached me at
Clyde, Wayne Co., N. Y., last Wednesday.
I had gone there to lecture, but a furious
storm of snow and wind, with the mercury
at zero, said I should not; so I didn't.
That night I sat four hours in a dépôt,
waiting a belated train, and next day
wended to Perry, N. Y., where the mercury
stood 26 *below* that morning. The last nine
miles made by sleigh, and I was called at
four next morning, to make six miles more
in an open cutter to meet a train at six
A.M. so as to reach my next appointment
without mistake. Then three hours more of
waiting (from ten to one) at a dépôt to
catch a train that would take me home.
And this broke down at Albany next morning, so that I had squandered my night to
no purpose. My friend, in the good time

coming, when women are' to do everything, get elected sheriff if you can, but don't try lecturing. It is too slavish. I *must* be counted out of it very soon.

*   *   *   *   *

I have a letter from I—— to Dec. 1st. She was then hoping to get away by herself for a three weeks' run down to Italy, as I barely hope she has done ere this, for I apprehend mother would decline to spare her when the moment came. I will enclose you G ——'s last letter, which you may return at leisure.

And so my sixtieth Christmas is going soberly and with abundance of work. I am no richer, unless in friends, for my last ten or twelve years' of hard work; and I begin to long for quiet and rest. I have hardly known what home meant for years, and am too busy to enjoy anything. I most regret the lack of time to read books. I hope I shall not die so ignorant as I now am.

I called on Mr. Barnum yesterday, and walked to church with him. He seems as well as ever.

And so, with fervent Christmas wishes for your happiness, I remain

Yours,

HORACE GREELEY.

XX.

NEW YORK, Jan. 9, 1872.

MY FRIEND: I have no excuse for inflicting my tediousness upon you, and will say nothing more of my perplexities. . . . "Nothing is so cowardly as Half a Million Dollars, except a full Million;" and it is a solemn truth. "How barely shall they who have riches enter the kingdom of God," is an awful truth. It does not appall me, because it strikes so far away; but I know how many it hits. . . .

I am rejoicing in the faith that my I—— is enjoying the holiday season in Rome, "city of the soul," which is her Mecca, and which she has long wished to visit. I do not *know* that she went, but presume she did about Dec. 20th. She was to go alone from Bordeaux to Nice, where she had friends who would accompany her to Rome. I presume she would find (or make) friends for a good part of her journey back.

They say that mother is very sweet and bright this winter, though unable to walk.

*   *   *   *   *

Yours,

HORACE GREELEY.

XXI.

NEW YORK, January 25, 1872.

MY FRIEND: Thank you for your last, which reached me on Monday afternoon, as I was leaving to lecture down East, whence I have to-day returned. I will keep out of politics* henceforth.

I send you two volumes of Browning, whereof I only expect you to read half. I know how subtle and obscure he often is; but then he is mighty when he is in his happy mood, and I wish you would read " Pippa Passes" some night when you are

---

* That is, in his correspondence with his lady friend. But his nomination to the Presidency compelled, very soon, a suspension of this resolution.—J. B.

all alone,—read it slowly, and let the fervor steal upon you gradually, like darkness. I judge that one reading will suffice.

Browning is a dramatist. "My Last Duchess" is but a fragment, but a fragment of a pyramid, a Tower of Babel. "The Blot i' the Scutcheon" is to be judged as a drama, not as a poem. If you will read "Luria" a second time I think it will pay. But a majority of the longer poems you will hardly be able to read once. And if you don't, no matter. The shorter poems are mainly simple and forcible. The "Cavalier Tunes" seem to sing themselves,—I mean they seem *to me* to do so. And, if you don't like anything else, you will oblige me by liking Browning's face. It pleases me better than Tennyson's.

I send you letters from both my children, because to hear from I—— in Rome is very much to me, and should be a little to my friends. G—— [is] taking care of her mother without I——.

* * * * *

I have much to do to-night, and will ask
you to excuse and believe me `

Yours,

HORACE GREELEY.

XXII.

NEW YORK, Feb. 5, 1872.

MY FRIEND: I believe Mr. J—— sent
you a card of invitation to his party on my
birthday; at least, I suggested it; not that
I expected you to come, but I fancied you
might like the card as a memento. I saw
Barnum among the surging crowd, and
would gladly have seen you on his arm,
but I did not expect it. I think he escaped
from the sweltering mass within an hour of
his arrival.

I had ridden all night from a lecture in
Maine, arriving late on a broken-down train,
in a blustering snow-storm. I worked all
day, and then stood up four hours shaking
hands. Going to bed just after midnight, I
found the muscles of my legs so swollen by
the unusual exercise that I could not lie
still without absolute torture: so I kept rub-

bing and moving them till daylight. They were nearly well last night, but I have had birthday enough to last me at least one year. Yet I ought to be grateful to my friends Mr. and Mrs. J——, who spent at least fifteen hundred dollars and turned their house upside down in my honor. If you did not receive a card, and would like one, I can get it for you.

I—— reached home [Arcachon] about January 7th. She says her flying trip to Italy cost eight hundred dollars, and was worth it. I am very glad that she has had it and enjoyed it. I wished her to leave Europe next spring content with America for evermore.

    *   *   *   *   *

I—— writes that mother grew stronger during her absence and now directs everything, though still unable to walk. They expect to come home next May.

Next week I must lecture all over Southern and Central New York,—which I wish were well over.

Yours,
HORACE GREELEY.

XXIII.

NEW YORK, Feb. 9, 1872.

MY FRIEND: I have yours of the 8th, which I shall not answer now, if I ever do, because I am writing this only to send you I——'s and G——'s letters just received, though the end of I——'s has not reached me. But what she writes is of no personal interest. I had asked her to bear witness that the massacre of St. Bartholomew (there called death of Coligny) is glorified in the Pope's Sistine Chapel of the Vatican, and, you see, she does it quite cleverly.

I thought I was alone in not receiving a card to that birthday party at J——'s, but you and some other friends seem to have been equally slighted. Be sure I shall get one, if possible, to send you as a memento of the event.

Please return my children's letters after reading them, and believe me, wearily

Yours,

HORACE GREELEY.

XXIV.

NEW YORK, Feb. 22, 1872.

MY FRIEND: I pray you never to call me by any other name than that my mother called me. I address you in that way, and wish to be treated as I treat others.

My lecture in F—— is next Saturday. But please do not go there, as I am to give an old lecture that you have already heard. If I ever give a new one near you, I will try to remember that you are to be notified.

I think Browning will grow clearer to you by patient reading. You *must* like " My Last Duchess," and " The Flight of the Duchess" is nearly as good. You already have read " In a Balcony" and " The Last Ride Together." Browning is more a dramatist than a poet, and does wonderful things when he really tries. The mischief is that he seldom tries. Let me owe you a letter till this headache goes off, which it can't till I have more rest.

Yours,

HORACE GREELEY.

XXV.

New York, March 13, 1872.

My Friend: I was glad to receive yours
of the 10th, even though it told me that
your mother had been severely ill (you remember that when I last saw you the question "Have we a healthy woman among
us?" was triumphantly answered by citing
her). She has already lived ten years longer
than *my* mother did, and mine was naturally
long-lived; but she was worn out before her
time. Your mother can hardly be left to
you many years longer, for sickness at her
age is serious.

You ask me as to a history of England
since 1700. I think Lord Mahon's comes
next in point of time to Macaulay's, but it
is too stately and political. Yet I wish you
would procure the first volume of Froude
and taste it. I read nothing but periodicals,
and know very little; but I once took up
Froude and read its best chapter,—a picture
of English every-day life under Henry
VIII., say about A.D. 1500,—and it delighted

me. I tried to do something like it in the
first chapter of my "American Conflict," but
fell miserably short, for want of time and
study and genius. If *you* read that chapter,
you will not stop there, but read more. I
guess Elizabeth was never dealt with severely
enough till brave Froude took her in hand;
while he is even *too* hard on Mary Queen of
Scots, demon though she was. I write from
hasty snatches here and there, mainly in
extracts given in reviews, but I feel sure
that Froude will interest you. The first
chapter assures me that he knows what history *means.*

You see that I am drifting into a fight
with Grant. I hate it; I know how many
friends I shall alienate by it, and how it will
injure the *Tribune,* of which so little is my
own property that I dread to wreck it;
yet . . . I should despise myself if I pretended to acquiesce in his re-election. I
may yet have to support him, but I would
much rather quit editing newspapers forever.

My folks have moved into Bordeaux, and
will soon leave that for Paris, in April, and

then London.   I hope to see them before
the 1st of June.

Yours,

HORACE GREELEY.

XXVI.

THE UNION LEAGUE CLUB,

NEW YORK, March 28, 1872.

MY FRIEND: I do not mean to write you
so often as I have done, but this photograph of my G—— is borrowed from her
cousins, to whom she sent it, and I cannot
keep it always, yet want you to see it.   I
learn that they had moved into Bordeaux,
and presume they are by this time in Paris.
I expect them all by the 10th of June.
Meantime, I want you to see how like her
is this picture of my girl.

You are right in not choosing to revive
the fearful memories of our late war; but
some time you will read Froude,—at least
the opening chapter,—and then I want you
to read the first chapter also of my "Conflict," so as to mark the difference between
the work of a great historian and that of a

little one. (I could have done better if I had not been hurried.) The fact that I never looked into Froude till eight years after my Vol. I. was printed will emphasize the coincidence in the scope and drift of the two chapters. But mine was dictated at a single sitting; his, I judge, was slowly elaborated, as it should have been. It is the best chapter of history that I ever read.

I was out of town yesterday, attending the funeral of a saint. She was of an eminent but decayed family, bred to genteel poverty, and was persuaded by relatives to marry a reformed reprobate, whose reformation did not endure. She has since endured fifteen years of exquisite misery, lighted only by one gleam,—her husband always honored and reverenced her. That was all the good there was in him. At length she died very suddenly, and I was glad for her when I saw her decently buried. Thank God for death, the one deliverer who never fails us! Yours,

HORACE GREELEY.

XXVII.

NEW YORK, May 1, 1872.

MY FRIEND: I have been very busy, and did not really mean to write you again just yet, but I have a letter to-day from G——, announcing the long-delayed start from Bordeaux, adding the . . . intelligence that she (G——) means to separate from the caravan at Paris and come home by herself this month. She has already forwarded by sailing-vessel direct a dog, which she enjoins me to feed on bread and milk and treat tenderly till she comes. I hope to welcome her within the next three weeks. Mother and I—— expect to stay till June, and may not come even so soon as that. I expect to find my girl much grown since you saw her, and even since I did, which was two or three months after. She had fever and ague when she left me, too sick to see her off, but she is now in excellent health.

I am kept at the office this week by the absence of my lieutenant, Reid, who has gone to Cincinnati. I am fighting a battle at this distance with the Free-Traders, who want to impose a platform on the Convention which will probably defeat its candidates. I am in their way, and do not mean to get out of it. They may make the candidate as they please, but not the platform if I can help it. I enclose you with G——'s letter my last telegram from Reid, as one of the curiosities of the canvass, which you may keep or destroy; but return me G——'s letter.

And so, with kind wishes for all friends, I remain   Yours,

HORACE GREELEY.

XXVIII.

[Copy of telegram enclosed in Mr. Greeley's letter of date May 1, 1872.]

To HON. HORACE GREELEY, *Tribune* Office, May 1, 1872.

If you are not nominated, I believe we can carry our tariff plank, remanding the whole question to Congressional districts. If you are nominated, the free-traders are

furious, and will demand something like
language of Missouri call. Last proposition
made to me by Wells is that exact language of New York call should be adopted.
I have said to Bowles, and others back me
in it, that they ought not to ask this of you,
but that it is barely possible that you might
not object to it. Pray telegraph me confi-
dentially on this point, if you can, to-night.
Small free-trade representation here from
New York fighting you bitterly in N. York
delegation.

WHITELAW REID.

XXIX.

NEW YORK, May 12, 1872.

MY FRIEND: If you look at the editorials
from Grant journals hurled from day to day
at the *Tribune*, it may strike you that I
am not highly esteemed by some of my late
compatriots, who ought to know me reasonably well; but you must consider that they
do not consider the matter quite so comic
as they would seem to. And then you

know that we quarrel more savagely with our ex-friends than with our natural enemies. My head is in such a whirl that I really can't remember whether it is Coleridge or some one else who says,—

Alas! they had been friends in youth,
*   *   *   *   *   *
And to be wroth with one we love
Doth work like madness in the brain.

But that is the truth. So be patient with my late allies, and hope that they will feel more kindly after a while.

There is one annoyance in my present position that I did not quite foresee. Not my having to submit in silence to charges that I could so easily refute; that is no more than I foresaw and was resigned to. But my glorious Saturdays are taken from me. A crowd of interviewers and daguerrotypists infest Chappaqua whenever I am expected there (also, in lesser degree, at other times), and make me stand against this tree, and on that ladder, and in this, that, and t'other absurd position, which they will soon be transferring to steam-presses and sending to excite the laughter of millions, who will of course suppose that I wished to be thus depicted and represented! Only one week a candidate, and already counting the time till I shall be out of my misery. I have news of the arrival of my folks in Paris about April 20th. G—— has decided to stay for, and return with, her mother and sister. A letter from my friend Mrs. C—— to our mutual friend General —— speaks of her as very handsome. . . . I hope the Cincinnati news will start them homeward before the end of May. I remain

Yours,

HORACE GREELEY.

XXX.

NEW YORK, June 3, 1872.

MY FRIEND: Our dear G—— has come back to me at last, but suffering sadly from typhoid fever. She was sea-sick for a day or two at the outset of her voyage, and then lapsed into typhoid, which rather increased on the way, as there was no doctor but a German whom she pronounced an ignoramus and threw away his medicine. After she landed on Saturday, by mischance after mischance, a full day elapsed before a doctor came to her bedside. I hope she is now doing well, but her eyes have a wild bad look, and she was wakeful and half delirious through the night. It will take weeks to bring her up, even if all goes right.

Her mother and sister are not sure as to their time of leaving Europe. Mother suffered from crossing the Channel, and is very infirm.

I am not well myself, nor likely soon to be. My weekly day of exercise and recreation at the farm has been spoiled by reporters and interviewers, so that I no longer regard it with pleasure or profit by it in health. We had a fine picnic there on the 25th, but I do not need picnics, and do need sleep, which hates to come near me. But the longest day comes to an end, and so it will be with

Yours ever,
HORACE GREELEY.

P.S.—I see that I am announced as invited to a clam-bake at your borough. Of
course I can't go. I should have to shake
hands with a thousand people, and that is
not a good exercise beyond the first five
hundred. My health is poor, and I want to
last at least six months longer.

H. G.

XXXI.

NEW YORK, June 16, 1872.

MY FRIEND : My folks came in yesterday
morning. I was over to Hoboken quite
early, for the Rhein had been telegraphed as
below, and went down the bay a short distance to meet her. My eyesight is so poor
that I did not recognize I—— among the
crowd of passengers on deck till long after
she had discerned me. Mother of course
was in her state-room below. They were at
the dock at nine A.M., and we were on
board soon after. The Rhein was a large,
rather compactly built village, numbering
about one thousand inhabitants, including

Strauss's famous band from Vienna, on its way to the Boston Jubilee, by which we were favored with several fine pieces, including the Germans' famous " Watch on the Rhine," as we came up the bay.

Mother looks older, thinner if possible, and has lost most of her remaining teeth since she left for Europe, Sept. 1, 1870, but she does not seem to have lost ground essentially. Her mind is as clear and her voice nearly as strong as then. We were two hours getting clear of the ship, but the fresh air of a June morning following a rainy night was very pleasant to her, after eleven days of ocean imprisonment, and she enjoyed the ride into and through the city, stopping at my sister's to have I—— see her sick sister, while the folks came out to greet mother. Then we made our way up to the St. Cloud Hotel, 42d Street and Broadway, because we have many friends living all about that point. Mother seems nowise the worse this morning.

I—— had terrible sea-sickness on the voyage, as usual, and her eye, which was nearly put out by a parasol in Rome last winter, broke out into fresh inflammation, but she is pretty well now. She will go up to Chappaqua in a day or two to make ready for her mother's coming. We hope to get up there in ten or twelve days.

G—— is gaining, but typhoid fever is very slow. It troubles us that she cannot be with us, but the doctor will not allow her to be moved, even from the room. But she will be with us at Chappaqua in a fortnight, I hope. And now, if you shall visit the city this summer, be sure to devote Saturday to us, and G—— will show you beauties that our place has not yet disclosed to you.

Yours,
HORACE GREELEY.

XXXII.

NEW YORK, July 1, 1872.

MY FRIEND: I—— and I got her mother up to Chappaqua on Tuesday last. It rained especially hard when we left the hotel and while we driving from Pleasant-ville to our place (two miles); but she stood it without complaint, and it was a sad pleasure to us all to see her once more in her own room and her own bed, where she seemed more contented and satisfied than she had done or could do at any hotel. She has had one or two severe attacks since, with difficulty of breathing, but, though she will never walk again, she seems as likely to live for years as at any time since 1865.

I—— feels a real relief in being at home once more, and, though overworked and most anxious, I hope her pallor will diminish and her strength increase as the summer wears on.

G—— was still in bed when we left, and not ready to come up on Friday when I called for her, but came up with the J—— family on Saturday. She is thin and pale, but no longer suffering, and took her place at our picnic lunch on Saturday as in the old days. I left her there on Saturday night, but she is coming down to-morrow or

next day and going up to Cooperstown with
the C——s at the close of this week. We
think the air of that high pure region will
be better for her than that of Chappaqua,
where we are still at our house by the village, which is our least desirable location ;
but mother insists on having the new house
plastered, etc., before removing to it ; and
that will about use up the summer.

We had quite a party on Saturday, and
our picnic in the pines (north of the garden)
was enjoyed by at least twenty. Some of
the guests contributed supplies, so that I——
did not bear the entire burden of preparation. We would gladly have gone to the
hotel, but she would not hear of it, though
her only servant left that morning and she
has not yet had time to get another.
She means to try a Frenchwoman who can
speak no English, so that she should hold
no communications with others except
through her. I am going to the Jubilee,
contrary to my own judgment and desire.
The pressure was at last so strong that it
would have seemed cowardice to hold off, as

in fact my chief reason for doing was a dread of making capital for my adversaries. In fact, my friends are so confident that we are to win the election that they prefer to try no experiments and take no risks. Still, I am going over to-morrow night.

You ought to see a few of the letters that I am favored with,—few of them asking outright for offices, but a good many asking for hats, as though I were a wholesale hatter. Three dozen assorted, is all that they require in the last of these missives I have opened. They are not among those I answer.

And so, with hope that we may see you and Mrs. R—— at Chappaqua before November (when I fear I—— will have to take her mother away by sea to some warmer climate), I remain

Yours,

HORACE GREELEY.

XXXIII.

MY FRIEND : I have yours of the 14th, and answer it at once, because I have hid-den where the throng do not find me, and have leisure that may not be mine another day.

I was not much interested in the Balti-more Convention. It did not seem to me probable that I should be nominated at Cin-cinnati, but I never doubted that Baltimore would accept the candidate of Cincinnati. There would have been no question of this if Cincinnati had nominated Davis, or Adams, or Trumbull. It was harder for the Democrats to take me, but there was really no alternative but the utter defeat and probable dissolution of their party. The medicine was nauseous, but the patient was very sick, and could not afford to gratify his palate at the cost of his life. The really astounding feature of the business is the adoption at Baltimore of the Cincinnati platform. Considering what you and I have known of Democratic hostility to negroes, negro suffrage, etc., it seems scarcely possible to realize that this is the same party that, barely ten years ago, so execrated the Emancipation policy and so howled at me when I addressed to Mr. Lincoln my "Prayer of Twenty Millions." It is hard to realize that this was barely ten years ago. I grow dizzy when I think of it. And I can imagine no reason for the adoption of our platform unless the Democrats (I mean the controlling majority) mean to stay on it. For they might have endorsed the ticket and spurned the platform. I have done so myself.

Whatever the result of the contest, the Liberal movement is a step in human progress. I do not believe it can ever be retraced.

Our I—— is overworked, but I see no help for it. The neighbors offer to help her provide for our visitors, but she will accept no help that does not leave her chief director She is thoroughly in the contest, and insists on doing her part in it. It would only annoy and humiliate her to interfere with this. She had about four hundred to feed last Saturday (a special occasion), and she had everything in admirable shape at a little before one P.M.

G—— is still in Otsego County, regaining her strength. She writes cheerfully.

Mother rode out to our picnic last Saturday, though she had not before been out of her room for weeks. She looked like a ghost, as she reclined in her carriage, but talked as if young and hearty. The day was very fine, and you know that our evergreens north of the garden afford the very place for a picnic.

You ask about "Parton's Life." It is a very crude affair, full of idle gossip which he picked up by inquiring at all the places where I had lived. Some of it is untrue; much of it is ridiculous. Still, as Boswell's Life of Dr. Johnson has supplanted the works of far abler and wiser men, I presume Parton's will be consulted so long as any shall care to hear or read about me.

I have been buried up in people for some weeks past, receiving calls almost constantly. It is a wearing life, especially at this season. Last evening I escaped under cover of a furious rain and came over to Brooklyn, where I am hid in a friend's house. This will answer for a few days; then I will take a new departure. I am going up to New Hampshire about August 1, to do a little quiet electioneering. So, you see, I am not likely to rust out very soon.

As to united or separate action, I guess the Liberals should organize separately, and then fuse at the proper time.

Yours,

HORACE GREELEY.

XXXIV.

NEW YORK, Sept. 10, 1872.

MY FRIEND: Having yours of the 7th, I write only to say that I trust you will not care what the result of our Presidential combat may be. Just now, the skies look dark; a month hence they may be brighter; but in any case I shall be what I am, and shall have less care out of than in office. Believe me in either case

Yours,

HORACE GREELEY.

XXXV.

NEW YORK, Sept. 11, 1872.

MY FRIEND: I have yours of the 30th.

Our G—— came down from Cooperstown last Thursday, and I took her up to Chappaqua next evening. She is quite recovered, though weak, and losing her hair. She is taller than when you saw her, and has recovered ten pounds of her lost flesh during her stay at Cooperstown.

I wish you had been up Kearsarge with me. It stands out by itself, in the heart of New Hampshire, with a circle of cultivated hill, valley, and woods all around it. Several lakes are visible from its summit. The ascent is very steep and difficult, but two or three young girls of half my weight and only a fourth of my years ran up it like goats. I had to rest repeatedly, and lay down on the summit. But the view from that summit is "a joy forever."

I am no more busy now than I always was, though seldom idle. I spent last Wednesday with Mr. and Mrs. Barnum at Bridgeport. B—— is as busy as ever, while Mrs. B—— is in better health than when we saw her together. I hope you may visit them here next winter.

I can't say about the election. The Grant folks are full of money, and are using it with effect. I shall do my best to defeat them, and hope to succeed. But defeat, should that occur, will have many consolations. I like my [home] better than any spot in Washington: wouldn't you? And while there are doubts as to my fitness for President, nobody seems to deny that I would make a capital beaten candidate. So let us trust that "He doeth all things well."

I was very glad to hear that Mrs. P—— liked us. I shall always like her, whatever she may think of me.

* * * * *

I rejoice that you know Oliver Johnson better than you did. He is pure gold; and when we meet, ask me to tell you of several whose behavior in the Presidential canvass has given me a better opinion of human nature.

With kindest remembrances to all our mutual friends in H——, I remain

Yours,

HORACE GREELEY.

XXXVI.

NEW YORK, Oct. 1, 1872.

MY FRIEND: Thanks for your letter just received.

As to the election, I am only anxious that my friends shall say after it is over, "He did not throw his chance away by any blunder. He *ought* to have won." If that is the general verdict I shall not object to being beaten. But I am not yet beaten.

I had a weary trip, having to be constantly on the alert. Usually, I drop asleep in the cars for a few minutes at a time;

but this time I was obliged to be con-
tinually on the alert. The reporters watch-
ing me compelled me to make different
speeches from place to place, while the
guns, drums, shouts, and hand-shaking were
a trial. But the general verdict of my
friends assures me that I did well, and that
contents me.

I go to-day to Kutztown, Berks Co., Pa.,
to talk on agriculture to-morrow, and must
hurry back at night to go to Riverhead,
L. I., to speak next day at another fair. I
could not get up to my little family this
week, though my wife's health is more criti-
cal. Such is my life. I hope to go home
next Friday night, but may not be able to
do so.

I saw A—— E—— at Bristol, Pa., and
Mrs. R—— at Cincinnati.

How I wish this was the 6th of November!   Yours,

HORACE GREELEY.

XXXVII.

NEW YORK, Oct. 14, 1872.

MY FRIEND: You must not take our reverses to heart. I may soon have to shed some tears for my wife, who seems to be sinking at last, but I shall not give one to any possible result of the political canvass.

I shall fight on to the end; but, for you, please say, with King Agur of old, "The bitterness of death is past," and think henceforth of less melancholy themes. Let us hold fast our faith in God, and realize that in a few years all will be the same, whatever the result of our present struggle.

Yours joyfully,

HORACE GREELEY.

XXXVIII.

NEW YORK, Nov. 8, 1872.

MY FRIEND: I have yours of yesterday. I write this because I wish to relieve myself of some bitterness, but do not expect—in fact, I scarcely desire—that you should

write me again these many, many days. I
am indeed most wretched. As to my wife's
death, I do not lament it. Her sufferings
since she returned to me were so terrible
that I rather felt relieved when she peace-
fully slept the long sleep. I did not shed a
tear. In fact, I am far beyond tears.

Nor do I care for defeat, however crush-
ing. I dread only the malignity with which
I am hounded, and the possibility that it
may ruin the *Tribune*. My enemies mean
to kill that; if they would kill me instead
I would thank them lovingly. And so
many of my old friends hate me for what
I have done that life seems too hard to
bear.

Enough of this. Speak of it to no one,
not even Mrs. R——, but return to cheer-
fulness and life's daily duties, forgetting, so
soon as may be,

Yours,

HORACE GREELEY.

[The above pathetic note is the last that
Mr. Greeley wrote to his friend and corre-

spondent. He died but a few days afterward, on November 29, 1872. The letter following was written by Mr. Greeley's correspondent, at a time, as the date indicates, previous to Mr. Greeley's nomination for the Presidency. The letter gives a picture of Mr. Greeley in his lighter and happier moods, and is well worthy of reproduction here.]

NEW YORK, April 29, 1871.

DARLING SISTER: Mrs. Barnum, Mrs. R.——, Mr. Greeley and I, are sitting around the centre table, the latter immersed in his letters, and the others talking about people I don't know; so I capture a sheet of paper and begin a note to you, to give you a little sketch of life as it has been with me since I came here. We reached New York about 12½ P.M., walked some distance to C. T——'s office in Broadway, thence rode in the stage up to Mr. Barnum's. There was a heavy shower on the way, but the sun shone out brightly when we reached the place, and taking that for a good omen I went in

cheerfully. Mrs. Barnum gave us a very
cordial greeting and took us down to lunch
as soon as our hats were removed. I spent
the afternoon resting and getting familiar
with the surroundings. Mrs. Barnum and
Mrs. E—— went out to ride, and Mrs.
R—— went to see Phœbe Cary, while I
settled down in a luxurious chair, with a
book for my companion, fell asleep and
awoke from it clear from the headache, to
my great relief. Punctual to the hour Mr.
Greeley made his appearance, satchel in
hand, and informed Mr. Barnum he "proposed staying in that house as long as those
ladies did." We had a very pleasant evening. Mrs. B——, of Boston, (who returned
with Mrs. R——,) A—— and L—— C——,
P—— and husband, and Mr. E——, were at
dinner, besides those I have mentioned, 14
in all.

Saturday morning, at 9 o'clock, we left
the City Depot for a trip to Chappaqua.
Only Theodore Tilton and wife were of the
party besides Mrs. R——, Mr. Greeley and
myself. Mrs. Tilton I fell in love with at

the first glance. She is a frail little creature, about your size, and is just coming back to life out of a long sickness. She looks up into your face with such loving, sincere, trustful eyes, that you feel like kissing her every time you meet their glance. The day was one of the happiest I ever spent in my life. Dear old Horace's face fairly beamed with happiness. We rode all over " Mother's land," up hill and down ravines, and over to see his woodland where he spends every Saturday chopping. He and Tilton kept up a fire of jests, and I looked at everything, and listened and enjoyed it all. How often I wished for *you!* I felt as if you was by whenever I drew near Mrs. Tilton, and more than once I addressed her as " Dolly," before I thought. There was lots of *fun* aboard. I'll never say again Mr. Greeley isn't *queer.* He drove slow, of course, and *such* driving you never saw. His old horses knew him, no doubt, and they paid not the slightest attention to his chirps and gentle shakes of the lines. He held one line in each hand, with elbows sticking out, and his hat on the back of his neck, while his horses went all ways but in the road, and sometimes took us over stumps, to the no small risk of an upset. We visited the cascade last, and drank from the spring as in duty bound. Mr. Greeley has firm faith that this is the very purest and sweetest water in the world. Tilton laughed at him for stepping backward into it in the morning, but Horace avowed it did not wet him at all, for he "drew his foot out so quick the water never found out it was *thar*." From thence we drove up by the field Mr. Greeley is so proud of, which "used to be the wickedest frog-pond you ever saw, all covered with miserable, useless hassocks and skunk cabbage, and so springy you could not walk over it in safety." It is a beautiful field now, but the old man's face, beaming in pride of it, was much more attractive to me.

Back to the house, we sat a few minutes before the fireplace and looked at the fire of that precious, dry red cedar, then over to the hotel to dinner. Mr. Greeley lamented much we could not dine at his house, and told me more than once, in a confidential way, it was "a sight worth seeing to see I—— get dinner there." Do you know, they have built *three houses* on the place, and only one of them is inhabited ; the man who farms using the back part of that. Besides, he and "Mother Greeley" each have a barn. Mrs. G—— would not have a tree cut, not even to trim it, about the first house. So they left that, and built another in the sunshine to be more wholesome. This second one was the one we entered, but they now have another partly built, which they propose to use if Mrs. G—— ever returns, as he thinks she will in the fall. They have lots of old stock about, which they keep for the good they have done ; as old cows, which "Mother says shall never be killed while she lives, because they have given milk to her children." They "fell down sometimes, and wanted to die, but Mother would not let them, and kept a man to lift them up and care for them." . . . We rode over to Sing Sing and took

the cars there to return to the city, which
we reached just at sunset. We rode home
in a carriage, had tea, and then Mr. Greeley
told us to come up into the sitting-room,
when he produced some books from his
pocket and read poetry to us all the evening. The first was Whittier's " My Psalm."
Read it, and see how appropriate it was to
close such a day. He took "Jim Bludsoe "
from his pocket-book and gave us that for
one selection. Out of paper and cannot
write more.

M——.

REMINISCENCES OF
HORACE GREELEY.

REMINISCENCES OF HORACE
GREELEY.

FEW characters in America have been taken so warmly into the people's heart as the editor and founder of the New York *Tribune.* In his day, which still seems so recent, though half a generation has now elapsed since his death, he was perhaps the most vigorous personal force at work among us. He had eccentricities and sharp opinions, which were the subject of merciless combat; but those who knew him intimately and best could pass these by, accounting them nothing against the genuine sincerity, the robust honesty, and the practical benevolence which he so abundantly illustrated. In his middle and later life, when he was the most lavishly abused and most widely talked about of any American per-

sonality, he had hundreds of warm friends
who held almost every opinion which he
condemned, and who, although they kept
this comment and criticism going, would
have sworn in court, if called upon, that
anything personally derogatory to him which
they had uttered was purely Pickwickian.

In any serious sense no impeachment of
his character would have been credible to
even his worst political opponents who
really knew him. Many of those, indeed,
who were hurling the most sturdy epithets
against him and his paper were often to be
seen walking and amicably talking with
him on the street, or entertaining him in
their private homes, as if Damon and
Pythias had come back once more. For
one winter at least, curious though it may
seem, he actually boarded with the family of
one of the leading editors of the paper which
was perhaps the most conspicuous party rival
of the *Tribune* in New York. Mr. Greeley
and this editor were for years attached
friends, and they must have read daily at
their common breakfast-table words on the

fourth page of their respective journals that,
spoken by two average persons in the street
by or of each other, would at once have provoked a fight. How they must have smiled
in their sleeves as they read them together
over the buckwheat cakes and steaming
coffee!

But Mr. Greeley began his editorial career
when euphemism and the "our esteemed
contemporary" style were not in vogue. It
was the fashion in the early days of newspapers not only to call a spade a spade, but
to load the handle of it also with no am-
biguous epithets. He had cultivated a
strong Saxon style all his life, as transparent
as Franklin's, as blunt and pointed as Cob-
bett's; and no reader ever laid down an
article which he penned with the slightest
doubt in his mind as to what was meant by
it. He was the last representative of that
personal journalism which made editor and
paper one thing. The plain country reader
always religiously believed that Horace
Greeley wrote everything that was printed
in the *Tribune*, unless it was the signed let-

ter of some correspondent; and there were
those even who, not very long before he
died, used to ask him when they met him
on his lecturing tours when their subscrip-
tions to the paper would expire! I am not
sure but he might have known how to answer this question occasionally; for he had
a wonderful memory at command, and could
tell you how certain obscure towns and
counties voted on many previous elections.
No such easy and friendly relation is now
maintained by a great paper with its patrons
as that which Mr. Greeley kept up even to
the very last years of his career, and it will
be impossible to behold again another editor
at once so great and so familiar.

My personal acquaintance with Horace
Greeley extended over the last fourteen
years of his life. Once he passed through
the town where I lived when I was a youth
of boyish enthusiasm, and lost his spectacles,
which were found and returned to him the
next day. The event was a memorable one
for a rural community where the *Tribune*
had so firm a hold, and greatly impressed

those who saw him, and piqued inquiry among those who, like myself, failed to get a view of one we considered so great. I should have been much surprised then to be told that in a few years from that date it would be my office and privilege to intro- duce him to a public audience there, and to repeat the performance very often.

On the first lecture occasion for which I engaged him, he came in the month of March to conclude the winter's course. It was the first course the village had ever had, and if it had not been for Mr. Gree- ley's name and fame it would have been the last so far as some of us were concerned; for, in spite of good names and good en- tertainments, the enterprise looked likely to end with disaster and a sizable debt. I even went to the hall with Mr. Greeley not without forebodings; for we depended mainly on the outlying country for our suc- cess, and the roads were as deep with mud and as impassable as March ever makes them. But the house was packed. It was as if an election were being held and a bugle-call to the faithful had been blown forth by the *Tribune*.

Mr. Greeley was not an orator in any scholastic sense. He had a poor and somewhat squeaking voice; he knew nothing of gestures; and he could not take an orator's pose, which adds such emphasis sometimes to the matter and argument to be set forth. Not all his years of practice on the platform and on public occasions ever changed his habits and methods as a speaker, and he ended as poorly equipped for the vocation as he was when he began it. But he had one prime quality without which all the others are exploited in vain. He invariably had *something to say;* and he said it in such clear and wholesome English, with such utter sincerity, with such humane endeavor, and backed by such a character for probity and guilelessness, that he was an orator after all, in spite of all the rules. I have introduced Wendell Phillips, George William Curtis, Anna Dickinson, and, in fact, all the most famous speakers of both sexes, including P. T. Barnum, Mark Twain, and Josh Billings, more than once and to various audiences, but no one of them ever gave better satisfaction, different and notable as they were, than Horace Greeley. As a consequence he came to me oftenest and wore the best.

We might, or might not, agree with some of his peculiar premises; as, where he says, "The moment a drop of alcohol is received into the human stomach, the stomach recognizes a deadly enemy," but he set his audience thinking and illuminated his theme.

At the conclusion of his first lecture in our village, when we were struggling to sustain the course, I was surprised, as I had not informed him of the situation, to hear him say:

"I want nothing for my services. Your town is small, and your association can not afford money for these things."

"But," said I, "Mr. Greeley, this was true enough when you came, and we expected to pay you nevertheless. But it is no longer true. Our receipts from your effort not only clear us from debt, but there are about sixty dollars left."

" Well, you will want that," he replied, " for next year."

Only by the strongest insistence could I make him take a fair remuneration, and by telling him that when we were deeply in debt again we would consider his generosity. One thing that I said to him, and which deepened his habitual smile, was to the effect that there was a very grave reason why he should take the money.

"My friend Mr. C. and myself," I remarked jocosely, " who are really the whole Lecture Association at present, are the Democratic Committee of this town, and if you leave this money in our hands, I am afraid it will make deplorable havoc with the next election returns."

Mr. Greeley was very thoughtful in making up his opinions, but very tenacious of them when they were once formulated. He imbibed his philosophy of a protective tariff early, considering it a benevolent remedy for the poorly paid agriculture which dis-

tressed him in his New England boyhood;
and he probably never varied in a small
degree even his opinion on that subject.
Nothing that was ever said by a free-trade
writer or speaker, I suspect, much disturbed
his faith. The paternal aspect of government, the enlargement of its forces for
doing good, chimed well with the ideas of a
philanthropist. All his opinions were rooted
in an earnest desire to do humanity good,
whether the means were wisely adapted or
not; and, of course, his views on slavery
and temperance were conspicuously philan-
thropic.

I remember well the first question he put
and his surprise at its answer, when he visited our leading agricultural store. He
asked the accomplished youth, who was
one of the firm, and who was also an accomplished farmer, to let him see one of
his subsoil ploughs.

"We do not keep them," was the reply.

"What! you pretend to sell agricultural
implements," said Mr. Greeley, "and don't
keep subsoil ploughs?"

He thought a blacksmith might as well be without horseshoes, for subsoiling was his special hobby. He instanced the deep tillage of Belgium and England, and said our only help now in agriculture, our best remedy for wet seasons, and for drought too, is to turn a deep furrow. It was cheaper, also, to extend our furrows downward than to buy land adjacent, and it served a better purpose. It affected him little to say that this was putting the rich surface out of reach; and that some subsoils no farmer could afford to turn up, or could make rich if they were turned up, for he had his answer to all this.

If he settled his philosophy of *things* once for all, his opinions of *persons* were occasionally more fluctuant. At one time when the Legislature at Albany was particularly malodorous, he told me after it adjourned that one of the members came down to the *Tribune* office during the session and piously lamented in pathetic terms the deplorable state of things there. He even wished that Mr. Greeley would say something about it

in his paper. Mr. Greeley was deeply impressed with this, and very naturally, as any
one of us would have done, left out this
exemplar of Spartan virtue from his denunciations. This was, in fact, the result
the "Spartan" law-maker wished to effect
by his visit to Mr. Greeley. "I thought,"
said Mr. Greeley, "this man who came to
see me was honest and straight, but, Mr.
Benton, he was the worst of the lot. He
went in, in all the steals, up to his armpits."

It was my privilege to elicit from Mr.
Greeley, in June, 1871, one of his first public utterances as a speaker, on the manage-
ment of Southern affairs under the carpet-
baggers' *régime.* I threw open our public
hall, and he spoke without notes. He had
already intimated, in letters written from the
South, the monstrous doings of the imported
officials in the lately disaffected States, saying that they were diligent in praying, but
they spelled *pray* with an *e.* His course
from this time generally led him, without
his thought or wish, to the Presidential candidacy of the next year. A failure though

it was at the time, it marked the parting of
two ways and left a profound influence on
the political thought and platforms of both
parties down to this time.

Mr. Greeley was a delightful man to talk
with, to ride with, or to be with in his intervals from active work.   He had been a
life-long reader in all directions, and, unless
you discussed the structure of languages,
which he had not learned, or something like
the Greek particle, or the dative case, you
would find him at ease with any subject.   I
once asked him if he had ever read Thoreau's address before the Middlesex County
Agricultural Society, Mass., in which he puts
forth his theory explaining why oak forests
succeed a grove of pines, and *vice versa*,
which I thought was of a nature to interest
him.   "Oh, yes," he said, "I have had a
long talk with Thoreau about it."   His
piquancy as a talker came not merely from
his fulness of thought and his ease in putting it forth, but the charm was heightened
by his remarkably polite manner as a lis-
tener.   He never dominated the company or

forced the theme. But he had an unfailing fund of matter at hand for its illustration.

A good many will be surprised to know that Mr. Greeley, whose prose style was directed to the understanding rather than to the imagination, was an ardent admirer and student of the best poets. They will be still more surprised to know that his favorite poet was not Pope, or any one like him, but Robert Browning. Swinburne was, perhaps, the next in order, or nearly so. I have heard him, when we were riding together, repeat whole passages from Swinburne's lyrics, those liquid and sonorous ones, like the song of " Dolores," being employed for this purpose. He seemed to enjoy the verbal melody, too, which was the probable cause of the recitation. My copy of the " Atlanta in Calydon" he retained for a year in order to find time to acquit himself of it.

At the time Mr. William Morris issued the first stout volume of his " Earthly Paradise," I happened to meet Mr. Greeley on a railroad train, and we sat in the same seat. I had a copy of the book in my hand, and he looked at it with some misgivings as to its dimensions, but soon saw enough of its quality to hope to be able some day to read it. When I told him that that was but a small part of the contemplated work, he exclaimed "Oh, Lord!" and gave up, in despair of making the author's acquaintance.

Once, at my father's house, where I usually. entertained him, he took up a volume of the poems of Uhland in the original. He studied out the similarities of some of the German words to their English counterparts with interest, and did not hesitate to ask an occasional question when it was necessary. I called his attention to a copy of one of Richter's stories, which was translated, but he had evidently tried this author some time to his disgust. The style was odious to him. Richter, he said, in substance, begins in the clouds and never gets out of them. His sentences have no conclusion and lead you nowhere.

At Chappaqua, on the Saturdays, which were regularly devoted to his farm, you were fortunate to be invited. He enjoyed the outing there as a boy would let out of school. The axe was the first thing asked for, and, when it was mislaid, nothing was done until it was recovered. Chappaqua is a little hamlet on the Harlem Railroad, about thirty-three miles north of the New York City Hall, which is opposite the *Tribune* office. He used to reach it an hour before tea Friday night, but he would often spend that hour in the adjacent woods with his axe. He was greatly like Gladstone in his choice of exercise as well as in a certain kinship as a publicist. Neither of these men affected chopping wood at the door or for fuel; but felling or trimming up trees was their peculiar delight. I have been with him when he would hand me a fresh magazine and fix a place for me on the rocks when he went in the woods to chop, saying, " Now I shall be near by, and you can talk or read as you like."

Everybody who has been at Chappaqua remembers the picturesqueness of the Greeley farm, and the beauty of the woods, the deep ravine, the stream flowing through it,

and the broad meadows, rescued from a
swamp by drainage, below. It has a number of springs at accessible points, where
Mr. Greeley used to stop and drink, rarely
skipping one as he went along. A tin cup
adjacent to each might be found always,
when no ill-intentioned wayfarer had spirited
it away. Once I amused him exceedingly
when a cup was missing at one of the
springs, by folding up a capacious leaf, and
improvising a cup from it, from which we
both drank. He had no idea so simple a
trick could be done.

I am sure manual dexterity is something
to which I can lay but the feeblest claim,
but now I think of it, I do not remember
that Mr. Greeley ever exhibited it even in a
primitive form. No utensil on the farm was
ever constructed or repaired by him, I imagine; nor had he any faculty, you would
observe, in a mechanical direction. He
could chop down a tree, but more often his
work was trimming the trees up and cutting
away the underbrush on the hill-side. He
often pointed with pride to the tall branch-

less poles in his woods, from which the ship-builders might select their masts, if occasion demanded.

I once asked him, when he was vigorously at work there in May, cutting down the alders full of sap and leaf, if spring was not the wrong season for that kind of work. And I mildly suggested that if they were cut in the fall his toil would be much more effective. But he said: "*Now* is always my time for anything. Pretexts for putting off work are the lazy man's argument." He had a fondness for forests, as if the spirit of the Dryads had somehow infected him.

He was proud of his meadow, converted from a swamp, but the woods he worshipped. He bought eighty acres of timber land, I think, at one time, and sowed the portion that had been deforested with locusts and chestnuts. He thought that every barren knoll or rocky summit that the plough could not ameliorate should be sown or planted with trees.

His habits on the farm were simple in

the extreme. A bowl of bread and milk was usually the first meal partaken of. In the city he indulged frequently in what we may call cultured cooking—the French *cuisine*—and seemed to enjoy it. I do not think it was ever true that he was a Grahamite in his habits, except experimentally for a brief period in his earlier career. At any rate, the first meal I ever saw him eat was an utter surprise to me, from the fact that it flew in the face of all the health rules from Moses down. Graham or Trall would have considered it next to a death-warrant to have partaken of it. During his convalescence from a brain fever, contracted in the dark days of 1862, a lady suggested to him that he should drink tea, which he had not been accustomed to. He did so and found it beneficial. It may be that his diet was widened a little after this recovery. Once he told me that his hand trembled, and he charged the disability to coffee. He at any rate dispensed with that drink, and found his nerves quieted by the change.

Mr. Greeley's sense of humor was of a

peculiar sort, but it was allied to genius. So many anecdotes have been told of him in illustration of this that one can hardly expect to reproduce any now that some one has not repeated. Those who tried to joke with him to his disadvantage were generally worsted, whether they did it orally or through the press. One evening an associate editor of the *Tribune* accosted him as he came in to his desk with some such question as this:

"Didn't you know, Mr. Greeley, that you made a dreadful blunder in one of your statistical editorials this morning?"

"No; how was it?" said Mr. Greeley.

. "Why, you said something about 'Heidsieck *and* champagne.' Don't you know Heidsieck *is* champagne?"

"Well," said Mr. Greeley quietly, "I am the only editor on this paper that *could* make that mistake."

On another occasion a person who wished to have a little fun at the expense of his consistency, said in a group where Mr. Greeley was standing:

"Mr. Greeley and I, gentlemen, are old friends. We have drank a good deal of brandy and water together."

"Yes," said Mr. Greeley, "that is true enough. *You drank the brandy*, and I drank the water."

Tobacco was his especial dislike; and, a friend of mine knowing this well, while handing around a box of cigars to a few who were present with Mr. Greeley, took especial pains to hand him the box with great ostentation.

"No," said Mr. Greeley, "I thank you. I haven't got so low down as that yet. I only drink and swear."

I must say, however, in contradiction of a charge that must have been much exaggerated and purposely distorted (for it was a favorite imputation against him with many), that I, at least, never heard him use expletives that could not be repeated in a refined circle. He had as justifiable occasions, though, for objurgatory epithets as any one I ever knew; and, if he had not sometimes spoken vehemently he would have been truly angelic. His handwriting, in spite of all that was said of it, was not the worst in the world; but it was very nearly the homeliest. It was fairly appalling to look at. But it *did* have a somewhat uniform alphabet. Almost all the words, like a certain one in Rufus Choate's penmanship, looked like "gridirons struck by lightning." But when you once discovered the key to this chirography, it was not so very hard to read. The stories about it, though, are more numerous than the fables of Æsop.

There is one impression about Mr. Greeley that is widely disseminated and vaguely accepted by a general consensus, that is far from being true. Every now and then you hear some one say that grief over his defeat in the presidential election killed him. I believe I have a peculiar right to form an opinion on this subject, for the same presidential election very nearly killed me. The campaign of '72 was a very long one, for one thing, and the summer was phenomenally hot. The Cincinnati nomination was made in the middle of May, and Mr. Greeley, in addition to the burdens it threw on him, continued for some time to fill his editorial place. He also tried to answer bushels of letters personally. He gave up the editor's chair, to be sure, after a little period; but he was writing all the while for a prominent cyclopedia, or travelling and writing speeches. When he made those twenty or more daily speeches in the fall, which pretty nearly broke down the young reporters who followed him to put them in order, his wife was on her death-bed; and for six weeks he had not slept on her account one night of natural sleep. Many nights an hour of sleep was all he got. For some years malaria had undermined his system; and, though it was wonderful what it bore, it could not resist everything. If his wife had lived, I am certain this shower of disasters would have fallen inert, although they were enough to kill two or three ordinary persons. It is the height of absurdity, therefore, to say that a man who always was boldest and most aggressive when in the minority, succumbed to a sen-

timental disaster which a minority precipi-
tated. There was only a brief period when
his chances of election seemed fair. I saw
him many times when they were doubtful;
and I know he was prepared for the worst
result.

His benevolence was always larger than
the public knew. His benefactions will
never all be known. He could not resist
appeals to his charity, whether they were
for a church or other cause, or for a person.
He put himself often to the greatest incon-
venience to lecture for some cause, *free*,
when the cause was much better able to
give him the fifty dollars earned than he
was to proffer his aid. I know one man,
not now living, who was in his debt at one
time fifty dollars incurred by separate dollar
gratuities. He was constantly lending out
money in this way. If he had had an eye
to money-making, or had been a trifle mis-
erly, he might have been a millionaire long
before he died.

Much was said in his early days of the

old white coat. It was not a mythical gar-
ment. It was hunted out of an old closet
once for my benefit on a midnight ride, and
when I wrapped it once and a half about
me, I was surprised at my own insignificance. Although the white hat and coat of
early tradition fitted his temperament and
complexion, he did not make them peren-
nial. He often wore darker clothes, and
sometimes a black crush hat. His clothing
was generally of fine texture, but it was
worn free and loose; some would say
"thrown on." But, if one half of his collar
retreated from sight, or his round leather
watch-cord took a subterranean leave of the
surface over which it should flow, he would
not notice the revolt from order. At the
Delmonico Dickens farewell dinner, where
he presided, which was held on a Saturday,
and which compelled his return at night
from Chappaqua, I assisted a distinguished
Philadelphia gentleman in turning down the
collar of his coat, which stood up perpen-
dicularly, just as he was to proceed from

the parlors to the dining-room. But, however awry a single feature or more of his dress might be, he was himself always scrupulously clean. I never saw his white collar or cuffs otherwise than white. Dust and dirt did not stick to him, nor did the political mud of which he was so often made the target.

Mr. Greeley's head and face were striking in a remarkable degree. No one could look upon him without feeling the presence of a great personality. It was said that when Daniel Webster was in London, people who knew him not turned around to look a second time at him. Carlyle called him "a steam-engine in breeches." In a different way Mr. Greeley was equally impressive. His frame was loosely put together, as if the head bore it down; but he had an Olympian brow above that shambling gait. His benevolence shone forth in a beaming smile. His face was to the last as smooth and unwrinkled as a boy's. His manner was as fresh and unsophisticated as a

child's. He carried into mature life the
eager zest of appetite, and sense of pleasure,
which never could grow stale. Age never
put its full prerogative on him; and when
he threw off the week's cares and ambled
about his farm, he seemed to me always
like a boy of a somewhat belated growth.
His light hair was no more gray at last
than it was at first. Yet Tennyson's line
on Wellington fell not inaptly into his
mature description:

"O, good gray head, whom all men knew."

I shall always think of Mr. Greeley (as I
have already remarked) as one of three
great Americans, the other two being Franklin and Lincoln. He was not President to
be sure; but he was the maker of Presi-
dents, and, had it not been for him, Lincoln, beloved and famous, might to the end
of his days have been nothing more than
a faintly remembered Congressman. I couple him with these two men because the

three were not only among the greatest of
our own country, or of any country; but,
they were peculiarly dear to mankind. It
will be a long time, I fear, before we shall
add a fourth to this unique group. I doubt
if we shall ever have another so intrinsically
dear to pulsing, warm-hearted humanity as
was Horace Greeley.

J. B.

www.ingramcontent.com/pod-product-compliance
Lightning Source LLC
Chambersburg PA
CBHW020338030726
47496CB00007B/1928